WALK ON THE WILDER SIDE

WILDER ADVENTURES, BOOK 2

SERENA BELL

JELSBA
MEDIA
GROUP

Para Aimee, Chloe, y Milagros.

1

On the day my life goes off the rails, the first sign of trouble appears at 9:18 a.m. That's when my boss hands me a chocolate-frosted donut and a cup of coffee.

I stare at her, confused, because Hettie has never brought me anything before, even though we share an office in the children's department of the library. She's a petite Black woman with corkscrew curls, a no-nonsense manner, and an iron hand. A good boss, but not a donut bringer.

She delivers the bad news quickly, like an experienced nurse giving a flu vaccine. I've been laid off, effective next month.

My position has been replaced city-wide by a kiosk equipped with artificial intelligence that can recommend books to patrons and read books out loud to children.

I stare at her with my mouth open. "Are you serious?"

She winces. "I'm afraid so."

"Does the kiosk wipe their noses if they cry? Does it remind them to wash their hands after they use the bathroom? Can it shelve every book in the YA section without having to look up the series order?"

"I'm so, so sorry, Rachel." Her face softens with pity and apology. "You've been amazing. The perfect employee, on every axis. You work hard, you're good with the patrons—big and little, I can always count on you, everyone likes you. This has nothing to do with you. It's all about money."

"I know," I tell her, because she looks as miserable as I feel.

"We'll miss you so much, Rachel," she says helplessly.

She tells me to take the rest of my notice period as paid vacation and sends me home.

I'm not one of those people who has a ton of stuff to pack up. I leave behind the office supplies, because the library never has enough money for good pens or staplers, and grab my coffee mug, my water bottle, my lip balm, my photos, and the small sign that hangs over my desk.

Stick to the Plan! it says. Then, below, in smaller letters: *(First, make a plan.)*

Oh, God, this *so* does not go with the plan!

I toss the donut in the trash can—no appetite—and drive home in a blur of panic. I've never not had a job. From the time I was a little kid, I was a good girl: respectful, obedient, high-achieving. I'm careful. I pay my bills early. I toe the line. I make plans. (And stick to them.) I had my first job lined up before I finished my library science program, which was part of my master plan:

1. 4.0 in high school
2. College
3. Grad school

4. Great apartment
5. The library job of my dreams
6. Awesome boyfriend
7. Meet the parents
8. Get engaged
9. Get married
10. Have two point five kids (I can't decide between two and three)
11. Live happily ever after

Getting laid off feels like getting a C on a test I studied really hard for. I can't even bring myself to call my parents or my best friend Louisa, because even though I know I didn't do anything wrong ("the perfect employee," Hettie said), I still feel oddly ashamed.

Okay, I tell myself, as I circle for parking near the Somerville apartment I share with my boyfriend, Werner (step six). I got laid off, and that sucks. Tonight, however, I will be able to check off number seven on the master plan. I am meeting my boyfriend, Werner's, parents. And meeting the parents is the perfect stepping stone to number eight.

Werner's and my one-year dating anniversary is just a few weeks from now, and I've been fantasizing that he'll propose.

Candlelit dinner, champagne, a ring box, or, better yet, a ring atop a chocolate lava cake or a tiramisu... And Werner on one knee, eyes glittering with love, telling me that since the moment he first saw me at the college alumni event and crossed the room to talk to me, he's known that this was where we were headed...

Then a nine-month engagement, a spring wedding, a year

of getting to know each other as man and wife, and the two-point-five kiddos (step ten)...

(I will make up my mind by then. I'm not planning to deal in fractional kiddos, I swear.)

The layoff is a minor setback, I tell myself. As a step in the plan, it isn't even essential to the success of the next few steps.

Whereas meeting the parents is key. And—silver lining—the early dismissal today gives me plenty of time to finish cleaning the apartment and make a few pies. It's only 10:22.

I slide my Prius into a skinny parking space and walk the three blocks to the two-family where Werner and I live. As I unlock the door and let myself in, I can smell the roast I left simmering in the slow cooker. And the cleaning products I used this morning as I started the process of making everything perfect for the parent visit.

I take another step and trip over something, a pile of black slinkiness on the foyer floor, a tossed-aside heap.

Absentmindedly, I bend down and pick it up.

It's a short, black skirt with a lacy hem. Pretty. Sexy.

My mind stops, like someone jammed a stick into the spokes of the hamster wheel.

This is not my skirt.

And then I hear the sounds. Two voices. One low, familiar, grunting, the other higher-pitched, whimpering.

My brain races to provide any possible explanation except the obvious one. And part of me must not want to know the truth, because I start making up reasons I shouldn't walk towards the grunts and whimpers.

There might be an intruder in our apartment.

Werner might be doing something private (all alone) (by himself) he doesn't want me to walk in on.

A dying animal somehow got into our bedroom?

Or it's just the television.

Despite my brain's attempt to save me from the truth, my feet carry me inexorably toward the bedroom door, past a woman's blouse and Werner's shirt, both discarded on the floor. By now, my denial is morphing into a slow-growing rage. I turn the knob. Push the door open.

I see Werner's pale butt first. I recognize it, somehow, even though I've never seen it from this angle. I know what it's doing, even though I've never seen it clenching and thrusting like that. We're not the type of couple that uses mirrors or makes videos of ourselves. We have plain vanilla missionary sex under the covers, because that's how we like it.

That's how Werner *said* he likes it.

Right now, however, he is standing at the side of the bed, pounding into someone who is on all fours on his —our—bed.

"What the *hell*?"

That's my voice. Which is remarkable for two reasons. One: I didn't mean to speak. And two: I never swear.

Werner yanks himself free of the woman underneath him so fast I'm surprised he doesn't break something, er, valuable. Which offers me a totally different unwanted backside view—ugh.

It takes the owner of this view a little longer than Werner to realize what's going on, but when she does, she gasps and grasps for anything she can find to cover herself. Even so, as she clutches Werner's quilt to her body, tugging it off the bed, I catch the front view: lacy red teddy and breasts pushed up to her chin.

Is that thing *crotchless?* my mind demands to know, despite the urgency and absurdity of the situation.

I've never seen her before, which is *very* slim relief.

"Get out," I snarl at her, and, to her credit, she gets, grabbing her clothes as she rushes out. I can hear her beginning to cry as she removes herself.

I'm alone with Werner now. He's desperately trying to get himself back into his tighty-whities. I guess it's a survival instinct, covering up your parts when you've been caught. He's red and breathless and saying my name, begging me.

"Rachel, please, it's not what it looks like."

"I don't think that's even *possible.*" A weird calm settles over me. If someone turns out not to be the man you thought he was, can you fall instantly out of love with him?

If someone disappoints you completely, does he lose his power to break your heart?

Or am I just in shock?

Shock is the more likely option. But I plan to take advantage of the numbness and clarity of mind while it lasts. "You were having sex with another woman in *our* bedroom. It's exactly what it looks like."

The bedroom I never stopped thinking of as *his* bedroom, my mind observes.

Shut up, mind.

"Rachel, please, listen. You're the one who's meeting my parents tonight."

"Oh, my *God,* is that supposed to *help?* You've just shown me your butt. Literally! The butt of a man who'd have sex with one woman on the same day another one is cooking for his parents!"

"Rachel, please. *You're* the girl I want to marry."

Those words stop me cold for half a second. Because they are—were—the prize I coveted.

And then I come to my senses: Werner is not a prize.

He's a total and complete loser who just did the lowest thing a boyfriend can do.

"Sure." I barely recognize my voice. It is hard, dark, cynical. "She's just the girl you…"

But apparently I have used up my ration of curses this morning, and I don't finish the sentence.

"Rachel, listen to me. If you leave because of this, I'll never forgive myself. You're my perfect woman."

My perfect woman.

And what did Hettie call me at work today, just before I was replaced by a kiosk? *The perfect employee.*

Perfect.

Perfect.

What horse pucky.

This being perfect thing?

It's not working out for me.

2

H ow does a bad boy end up hosting a book club on his boat?

I've asked myself this question several times over the course of this wretched night. We're on my 30-foot fishing boat, currently anchored in the middle of Sentinel Lake. The sun has not yet dipped behind the mountains. The air is warm, the water still, the birds starting to sing. By most measures, I should be in my happy place.

Yeah. Not so much.

"You're out of toilet paper!" One of the book-clubbers, a whippet-thin, pale-skinned blond woman named Jennifer, pokes her head into the cockpit as she returns from the head. Jennifer has her mini-poodle-chihuahua mix—Chicklet—in a sporty sling-bag obviously made for that purpose. He has been intermittently yapping and whining, and I feel his pain —he's zipped up to his ears. "I used the last. Where do you keep the extra? I can swap it in."

"What do you mean, out of toilet paper?"

"I used it up," Jennifer says. "Also, the toilet's clogged."

I close my eyes. "You're kidding me. How many squares did you use?"

She shrugs.

"Didn't you hear me say four squares?"

She crosses her arms. "I thought you were joking."

I'd given all the book-clubbers a lecture about the perils of too-much TP in a boat head.

Which they had apparently ignored.

My jaw aches from clenching it.

Jennifer tips her head to one side. "Anyway, where's the extra TP?"

"There's no extra TP. That should have been enough TP for several book clubs."

"Seriously?" She raises two perfectly arched eyebrows.

"Seriously. And no one can use the head now. There's no way I can get that thing unclogged without a snake or a pump."

Jennifer makes a noise I'd translate as "harumph" and turns to join the other book-clubbers in the bow. I step away from the center console helm, intending to see how much damage she's done to my head, but before I even reach the cabin door, I hear a sharp *ziiiippp*, followed by yapping and scrabbling. I turn to see her freeing the doglet for a putter around her feet.

"Watch him," I say sharply. "I'm not going in the lake after him."

"Oh, is that service *extra*?" she snaps back. "Like toilet paper?"

I swallow my urge to engage, and go belowdecks. I take one look at the contents of the head—and oh, fuck, it definitely needs to be pumped. And is that—

Oh, no, she didn't.

Menstrual pad.

I rub my hand, hard, over my forehead, hoping the pad will vanish, but no such luck. Then, gingerly, I reach in and extract it with two fingers and drop it in the trash.

I wash my hands, frowning at myself in the mirror.

This trip is a total failure. There's no way to sugarcoat it.

And there's definitely no way to stave off the inevitable rotten reviews.

How was I supposed to know that I'd need more than two bottles of wine?

Or more than a small bowl of jelly beans and a big bag of Doritos? My clients finished both in thirty minutes and asked me where the refills were. One of them asked if I had any healthy snacks. Another wanted to know if I had sparkling water. I had to choke down the urge to point out the sun reflecting off the lake. *Sparkling! Water!*

Also, they hate the book, which is by some guy named Nicholas Sparks.

(I would not have chosen a book by a guy whose last name was clearly made up.)

The book choice is not my problem, but I feel like it's making the situation more dire. As are the mosquitoes—which have been worse in our area in the last few years.

I forgot to bring the nice-smelling bug wipes my brother's girlfriend bought for this occasion. Also, the sunscreen—Jennifer's nose is a scary shade of pink, and even with a couple of months of base tan on my white-boy skin, I'm probably hurting too.

I go back to the helm.

The women—my clients—are now talking about me in

whispers. Which, unfortunately, I can hear perfectly because of the weird acoustics of the boat on water.

"He was engaged to Zoë Milano, wasn't he?"

"Mmm-hmm. But he broke it off."

"I guess that's not a huge surprise, right? I mean, those tattoos and that leather jacket don't exactly scream *husband material*."

"They scream *something*. Or maybe screaming is just what any of us would do in bed with him?"

Lots of throaty laughter.

These women on my boat are all mid-thirties to early forties. They're the yummy-mummy type. If you'd asked me to assess them as they were climbing on board, I'd have said I wouldn't kick any of them out of bed. But right now? I want this night to end so I can get them off my boat.

I didn't used to mind being women's bad boy fantasy. But lately, I do.

Every woman wants to fuck the bad boy, but no woman trusts the bad boy to take care of her and the things that matter. It's a lesson Zoë knocked into my head.

I fidget with the fishing fly I keep in my pocket. It's one my dad made when I was a kid. He cut the hook off and let me keep it. Some guys have rabbit's feet, I have a "woolly bugger," with most of the feathers worn off.

"He's the baby's father, right?"

The fist that never quite leaves my chest clenches a little tighter. That baby they're talking about is Justin. My Justin.

Not my Justin.

"No," someone says. "He's *not*. That's what the fight was about."

I close my eyes, which is one of those dumbass things you

do when you really want to close your ears but it's physically impossible.

"Len Dix is the father."

The name physically hurts. Like a fishhook through the heart. Barbed.

"Wait. I thought *he* was the dad." *He*, meaning me.

"Zoë *told* him he was the dad."

If the news is out, it's only a matter of time before everyone I know—including all my family members—learns it, too.

I know that means I'm living on borrowed time. I need to tell them before they hear it like this, from strangers at a book club.

I can't take anymore. I start the engines, throw us into gear, and jam the throttle. There's a scream, a splash, and, "Chiiiiickleeettt!"

Shiiiiiit.

I guide us to the quickest halt I can and rush to where the women are leaning over the starboard bow, wailing and pointing.

Jennifer is wringing her hands and imploring her friends to go in after her doglet because she can't swim.

Chicklet, for his part, is treading madly, his bug eyes huge with panic, his little paws scrabbling, his nose barely above water. I whip my t-shirt over my head, shed my shoes—luckily, I am wearing swim trunks and not jeans—and dive.

Moments later, I deposit a shivering and coughing Chicklet over the side and hoist myself back in.

Does Jennifer thank me? No.

She hollers, "You could at least give a girl some warning! Chicklet could have died."

"If he fell in, he must have been on the gunwale."

"He wanted to see!"

I close my eyes.

"You started fast on purpose!"

"It's rude to gossip!" I roar.

I've shamed at least a couple of them, if the ducked heads are any indication. But it's a shallow victory, because Jennifer is *pissed*.

The reviews I desperately need?

Just got way worse.

And I can't even bring myself to give a shit.

Except I have to give a shit. All of us—the five Wilder Brothers—are working together to revamp our business, after our rodeo town became a wedding-and-spa destination— overnight. My oldest brother, Gabe, hired a consultant to guide us. The consultant—Lucy, who is now also my brother's new girlfriend—decided I should expand my charter fishing business to include other activities.

Like book clubs.

I want Wilder Adventures to rebound. I want it to stay in business. I want it to keep feeding my brothers and my mother and my sister Amanda and her husband and three kids and Gabe's girlfriend Lucy.

I want it to pay my salary so I can give Justin a good life, even if Justin isn't mine and I have to do it in secret.

So I have to figure out how a bad boy runs a book club. Or whatever it's going to take to make my part of the Wilder Revamp a success.

The women are murmuring among themselves now. I can tell it's bad news even before Jennifer approaches me. She's been appointed spokesperson, obviously.

"We think you should consider giving us all a discount on tonight's trip. Fifty percent off."

I grit my teeth, worried that if I speak I'll say something I'll regret.

What I finally say is, "That seems fair."

She's only slightly appeased. The wrinkles in her forehead don't smooth out at all. "You're lucky we aren't demanding a full refund. The snacks, the wine, poor little Chicklet, a clogged toilet, and *no toilet paper*?"

I want to fight back—there was plenty of toilet paper!—but I know it'll only make the review situation worse.

"I'm sorry," I say, instead, because my mother taught me the importance of a real apology.

I want to beg Jennifer and her cronies not to trash me in the reviews, but I can't bring myself to do it. Besides, I'm pretty sure it's a lost cause.

The bad reviews will suck, that's for sure.

But the worst part isn't the reviews.

It's what my brother Gabe will say about them.

"**W**hat the fuck, Brody?"

My brother has ambushed me from behind while my best friend Connor and I are cleaning my other boat. A small one, it currently sits on the trailer at Wilder Adventure headquarters, also known as the barn outside Gabe's house.

Spoiler: Jennifer and her friends' reviews did not mention that I rescued Chicklet from sure death. Only the lousy snacks, the bad attitude, the lack of toilet paper, and the rapid acceleration.

I slowly turn around to find Gabe standing there with a sheaf of printed papers and a furious expression. My own anger meter goes from zero to highway speed, because with Gabe it's always like this—there's nothing I can do that won't make him mad, and no way for me to win.

"What're you so pissed about?"

I try to keep my voice level, but it's a lost cause. Clark, Kane—even Easton—can keep their cool around Gabe. I'm the only sibling who loses it every time. It's because Gabe and

I are so close in age, and we had to compete from the very beginning for our parents' affections—a battle I gave up on winning sometime around sixth grade.

"This last batch of reviews—what the *fuck*, Brody?"

"We've already established that's the question," I say dryly.

There's a small snort of laughter that only I hear. Connor is hidden behind the boat, out of Gabe's view, which puts Connor in the awkward position of either being an eavesdropper on a family conversation—or having to pop out in the next few seconds like a jack-in-the-box.

He doesn't pop.

I can't blame him. I wouldn't want to show my face to Gabe if I didn't absolutely have to.

I wouldn't have chosen this morning to clean the boat if I'd known Gabe was around. I thought he was in Portland with Lucy, on a marketing research mission.

Gabe scowls. "You deliberately sped up the boat to capsize someone's dog? They want to know why you're bothering to offer these nights out, since you obviously have no interest in being a good host. I'd like to know the answer to that, too."

I only saw the reviews day before yesterday, but of course I've known this moment was coming since last Sunday. It's almost a relief to finally be here.

And I can answer his question, no problem: "I'm hosting the nights out because you told me to."

The red deepens on Gabe's face.

"I've had it up to here with you, Brody. Clark, Kane, Easton, they're all doing everything they can to make this work. Lucy's killing herself coming up with great ideas.

Books-in-the-Boat was a stroke of genius." He throws his hands out. "It's like you're hell-bent on undermining everything. Do you even give a shit if this business is successful?"

Of course I do.

That's what I should say. It's the truth. And those words might defuse this situation, especially if Gabe could hear how much I mean them.

But ever since I was the little kid in Gabe's shadow, part of me can't stand to let him win and have all the spoils and pats. So I do dumbass shit like this:

I shrug.

You can practically see the rage meter top out. His face turns even redder; his brows lower. He looks like a bull that's about to charge. And even though part of me feels like crap, another part of me scores a perverse thrill from getting to him.

Brothers, man. It's a fucked-up relationship.

"That's *it*, Brody. I'm done cutting you slack. If you don't get your act together and make this work, I'm cutting you out of the business when we allocate mom's shares."

My heart kicks up to a gallop. "You can't do that."

He crosses his arms. "I sure as fuck can. And I will. If you don't start bringing in tourist money and good reviews, I will. You have till the end of this summer, or I'm done with you."

He shoves the papers into my chest, turns, and strides away. The papers fall to the ground, where they're picked up by the wind and whipped into the trees. A moment later, he swings himself into his Jeep, revs the engine, and roars out of the driveway.

I stand there, a little stunned. More than a little stunned.

I didn't think he'd get *that* mad.

"Well, *shit*." Connor steps out from behind the boat.

I'd forgotten he was there. Always good to have someone witness your lowest moment.

Or your second lowest, anyway.

"He's *pissed*." Connor raises both eyebrows.

"Thanks, dude," I growl.

"You should have told him why you did it. Why you sped the boat up."

I'd told Connor the whole story, how they were talking smack about me and Zoë and baby Justin, and I lost my shit. Connor had hmmmed sympathetically. Connor has always been like that, a good friend no matter what kind of asshole moves I pull. I can't tell you how many times in my life he's been there for me after I blew up something that mattered to me—an exam, a class, a job, a relationship, my engagement. He always takes my side.

"You should tell Gabe the truth about Zoë and Justin."

I shake my head.

"Why are you protecting her? She's not worth it. After what she did."

"But Justin is," I say.

Connor gets quiet. He knows there's no arguing with me about Justin.

I realize I'm still holding a dripping sponge, and set it back in the sudsy bucket. "What was I fucking thinking, Con? Marriage? A lifetime commitment? Maybe for some guys, but not for me. I should just thank my lucky stars it imploded when it did." *Before I had a chance to fuck it up.*

"Maybe you'll feel different at some point," Connor says.

I shake my head. "No. I thought I could be that guy. A dad.

A husband. Whatever. Someone people could admire. But it's too much fucking work."

"You know, people do admire you." He thinks about it a second. "Except when you're capsizing their dogs and denying them toilet paper."

I think about this for a moment, then shake my head. "Not Gabe. If he admired me, he would have tagged me to run the business—or at least me *and* Clark—when he thought he might move to New York City to be with Lucy."

Connor doesn't try to argue, because he knows it's true. "You could make him admire you."

"How so?"

"What if you stopped fighting him all the time? If you did what he wants, instead of making him drag you kicking and screaming?"

The thought makes me want to hurl. Connor must be able to see that on my face, because it's his turn to shake his head. "Well, you don't have much of a choice at this point, do you? If you don't shape up, he's going to cut you off, and then what?"

"Then maybe I'll open my own business and not have to deal with his shit."

Connor squints. "Is that what you want?"

I think about it. My dad, my brothers, the business we built. About what it would mean to ditch out. About how it'd make me feel to be on the outside.

That makes me want to hurl, too. I shake my head. "No."

Connor paces back and forth a few times along the side of the boat, then slaps a hand on his thigh. "I have an idea."

"What's that?"

"My mom's got this new business. One of those sell-out-of-your home things. Beauty stuff, like body wash and perfume and shit. She does these girls' night parties. Women love them. My mom can't keep up with all the requests. I bet that would work for your boat. And my mom coordinates the food and wine and everything. You could redeem yourself without having to personally kiss a lot of ass. They do the party, you just supply the location."

Huh. I don't hate the idea.

"You'd still have to buy TP," he says, always practical. "And not forget the bug wipes."

"I can totally handle that much. Jesus, that sounds like a fucking dream. I'm all over that."

"The only thing is, my mom broke her foot, so I don't know about the whole boat thing."

"Well, shit," I say. "How'd she do that?"

"Stepped off the curb wrong in town, twisted it in the storm grate."

I wince. "That sucks."

"Yeah. But she said she was maybe going to ask Rachel to help her out, so I guess Rachel could do it."

You know the buzzer sound that signals the end of, well, anything? That's the sound that just zapped through my brain.

"Wait, Rachel's home?"

I try to make it sound like, "The Ducks have the early game?" or "You up for grabbing a pizza and a couple of beers?" but it still comes out sounding more like my sixteen-year-old self than I'd like.

Luckily Connor doesn't pick up on the fact that I just insta-reverted to my teenage years. "Yeah. Some shit hit the fan for her and she's regrouping."

Rachel is Connor's younger sister. Her hair is long and thick and not-quite-black. Her skin is a warm, light brown. She has dark brown eyes and a mouth that, in recent years, has made me think about blow jobs.

Okay, who am I kidding? Her mouth has made me think about blow jobs for way longer than I want to admit.

It's the lower lip. It's full and sulky and she licks it when she's nervous. I'm not sure whether it's the peek of tongue or the glossy sheen left behind that drives me so wild, but there you have it.

My life plan, since late high school, has been to avoid Rachel Perez at all costs, because that lip—her whole mouth, in fact—no, make that everything about her, inside and out— feels like a clear and present danger.

It is a threat to my sanity and, more urgently, to my friendship with Connor.

However, because life is what happens when you're busy making plans, Rachel is everywhere.

She saw me last month when Len Dix taunted me in Oscar's Saloon & Grill and I punched his lights out. She doesn't even live here; she just happened to be in town from the East Coast to visit her mother. They were taking a family ski trip for her mom's birthday.

And now she is, possibly, the only thing standing between me and a simple solution to my business problem.

Because I don't think my sanity would survive being alone on a boat with Rachel.

"Do you really think Gabe would kick you out of the family business?" Connor asks.

Right. In corner one, we have the threat to my sanity from

Rachel Perez. And in corner two, we have the threat to my livelihood *and* family life from Gabe Wilder.

Vegas has *no* idea where to put its money. God damn.

"You know what?" Connor says. "Forget I said anything. It's a bad idea."

"Wait, why?" I demand, although I'm pretty sure I know what he's thinking.

"I don't want you and Rachel on a boat together. She's a mess, and so are you."

I raise my eyebrows, and he clarifies. "She was waiting for her boyfriend to propose, and it turned out he was screwing another woman."

I'm already figuring out how to kill this asshole. My hands ball into fists. Whoever he is, he's going to die if I ever meet him.

"And you're still a mess from the Zoë thing. You're both hurting, and you know how hotheaded we all are when we're hurting."

Yeah, I do. I was a total rage-ball in the wake of Zoë's betrayal, and Connor was patient with me while I worked through a world of fighting and fucking. Well, mostly fucking. There was just the one fight. The one that Rachel unfortunately witnessed.

But yes, I do know how hotheaded we are when we're hurting.

"Give me some credit, Connor. I'm not a total dog."

He gives me a look that suggests this is in doubt. (Ouch.) Connor, like every other older brother I know, is insanely protective of Rachel. But if Connor thinks he's the only reason Rachel's off limits to me, he doesn't know me very well. Or, well, Rachel.

From the time she was a cute little kid, Rachel has always been a star student. A good kid, a model daughter. She has always had a life plan, and the idea that she would ever honestly want anything from me except what most women want—the bad boy fantasy—is laughable.

No. Rachel is safe from me, except in my dreams.

And I'll have to find some other way to save Brody's Boat and my relationship with my brothers.

"Rachel," my mom says. "I need your help."

I turn to look at her. She's sitting on the couch, both feet on the coffee table, soft cast resting on a pillow. She's propped up with all the other throw cushions and surrounded by books, her tablet for streaming movies, water bottles, and snacks.

"What is it, Mami?" I ask, ready to give her whatever she asks for.

Since I arrived back home, my mother has been desperately trying to snap me out of my funk. Smothering me with fragrant hugs. Cooking my favorite meals, fricase de pollo, carne con papa, lechon asado with all the fixings. She told me she never liked Werner anyway; he took me for granted (probably true) and had a stick up his butt. *That* comment caused me to have a terrible flashback to his rearview.

Finally, when all else failed to cheer me up, she introduced me to *Crash Landing on You*, her favorite Korean drama. Even though she was on episode thirteen and watching with me meant she had to start over.

Then a couple of days ago she took me to Rush Creek for retail therapy and broke her foot, because apparently Mercury is in an actual shame spiral.

Since then, our positions have reversed, and I've been doing anything I can to make her comfortable.

"Don't say no until you hear the whole thing."

Uh, oh. That sounds ominous. I take a deep breath, cross my arms, and prepare myself.

"I need you to help with my business."

"Your business?" I ask. To say I'm surprised is an understatement. My mom is efficient, busy, and organized, so, yeah, she *could* run a business, but I have never heard a hint about her starting one.

"You know your abuelita has been struggling a bit lately."

I do know. My grandmother is getting older, and both her knees are bothering her. She can't manage as well for herself as she used to, and my mother has been talking for almost a year now about moving her out to Rush Creek from New York City.

"I got an apartment for her," my mom says.

"Oh!" I say. "That's great!" I've almost forgotten that we're in the middle of a story that started with *Don't say no until you hear the whole thing.* I'm just incredibly happy for my mom and my grandmother, who have always been super close, even after my parents moved to Oregon for my dad's forest service job. Ever since I was a little girl, my abuelita has visited for a long stretch every year, and one of the reasons I've loved being on the East Coast is because I've gotten to see her more frequently. I'll be sad to be far away from her again —but it'll be worth it to know she's safe, well-looked-after, and near my mom.

My mom sighs. "But the budget's too tight, so I got a job. I'm doing sales. Like Josie does—with the essential oils, but this is more like body lotions and self-care items."

"You mean a pyramid scheme," I say, laughing.

She shakes her head. "No. This one's legit. No money up front, no recruiting bonuses, just healthy commissions. And I'm making good money. I just need to add more parties. I scheduled a bunch, but then, this." She points to her foot. "So I'm wondering. Do you think you could stay, just till it heals, and help?"

"What would I need to do?"

"It's not hard," she says. "You just need to be my legs, basically. You deal with food and drinks and carrying the bins of merchandise. You bring me things, and I'll do the talking. I know you want to get back to Boston as soon as possible—"

I shake my head. Yes, I want to go back to Boston—but there is no way I'm leaving my mom in the lurch. "Of course, Mami. Of course I'll help."

The doctor said five weeks to heal the foot, and almost a week has already passed. I can start the job-hunting process just as well here as in Boston. I won't have to look for an apartment, because Louisa is letting me sublet a room in hers.

I bet in another four weeks, I'll have stopped crying at unpredictable intervals, which will make me a much stronger candidate in job interviews.

My mom points a finger at me.

"And if you hear anyone at the Wilder party say 'self-care,' 'spa,' 'self-indulgence,' 'girls' night' or anything remotely in that category, point me in their direction. I need to double the number of parties I'm doing now to reach the goal I set for myself."

"Will do," I tell her.

The housewarming party at Gabe Wilder's is my mom's latest, and most blatant, attempt at cheering me up.

"Mamita," she said this morning, when she informed me that we were going, broken foot and all. My mom was born and raised in the U.S., and doesn't use Spanish much except when she's talking to her older relatives, but it shows up occasionally, especially in her favorite term of endearment. "Five Wilder brothers. You can't be in a bad mood when you're surrounded by those boys."

"Mami," I said sternly. "This isn't some get-back-on-the-horse thing, is it?"

"I don't know what you're talking about," she said innocently. "I wouldn't try to fix you up with a Wilder. Your brother would have my head on a platter. Besides. I know you. You wouldn't move back to Rush Creek if we paid you a million dollars. You couldn't wait to get out of here."

There's a note of sadness in her voice, but she's been amazing overall about the fact that I live on the other side of the country and can visit only a couple of times a year. Cuban families tend to stick close together, but since she and my dad moved far from family, she wasn't surprised that I did the same. And she's right about the fact that I've never thought about coming back.

It wasn't that I hated Rush Creek so much. It was *fine*. But I wanted to live in a city. And I have. Four years in Seattle, at the University of Washington, and then grad school in Boston, where I've stayed. At this point, I can't imagine coming back here for good. No: My plan is to regroup, dry my eyes, and go back to Boston with a job on the hook.

And that's still my plan—I'm just adding an item to it: *Get Abuelita to Rush Creek for Mami.*

MY MOTHER WAS RIGHT: The Wilder brothers are good for the soul.

I help my mom walk around the house and into the backyard, where the party is in full swing, and am blinded by the glare of all that Wilder beauty.

I grew up with them, but time has actually improved them. Picture the five best-looking white guys you can imagine, dressed for the summer weather in sporty shorts and t-shirts that look like they were custom made to cling to and drape over sculpted pecs, broad shoulders, and ridged abs. Five pairs of thickly muscled legs divinely graced with just the right amount of curly hair, and five pairs of strong, tanned forearms with more perfect brawn.

Actually, only four of them are here.

Clark—imagine a brooding Viking warrior, beard and all —and Easton—pretty boy to the stars, with a smile so high-wattage he probably doesn't need charcoal starter—are manning the grill, drawing a small circle of chatty women. Easton is managing them like a trained pro, because Clark doesn't talk much these days, and he definitely doesn't flirt—not since his wife passed away last year. Gabe—tall, dark, handsome, and commanding like an outdoorsy Mr. Darcy— is circulating with a pretty blond I recognize as his new girlfriend. And Kane—boy-next-door handsome and kind to everyone—is helping a few kids roast marshmallows over a small fire pit.

Brody Wilder, who also doubles as my brother Connor's best friend, is not here.

And believe me, I noticed.

Anyone would. It's like the Wilder set is missing its "bad boy" paper doll.

I can't decide how I feel about Brody's absence. On one hand, I've had a crush on him since I was, I don't know, six years old, and fantasizing about him has given me hours of personal entertainment.

On the other hand, if Brody's not here, he can't make me feel like a speck of dust clinging to the side of a mountain merely by not noticing that I exist.

Tough call.

I greet all the present Wilders—four brothers, their mom, Barb, and—

"Rachel!!!"

Amanda Wilder flings herself into my arms.

We give each other one of those rocking, shaking hugs, and then she checks me out all over like she's making sure I'm still intact.

I feel like the answer is *barely*. But a little better each day.

"How are things?" she demands, and then, before I can answer, "How long are you in town?" and then, "When can we get together?" and then, "Crap, follow me, I have to chase Kieran."

I do, and three-year-old Kieran, who like both his siblings is obviously in training to become beautiful like his mom and uncles, takes us on a jog to the front of the house, where he climbs into the rocking chair on the front porch and announces that he's riding a horse.

"Thank God—that will keep him still for a few minutes," Amanda says, out of breath, laughing. "So, now. Tell me everything."

"I don't know where to start," I say, laughing, too, because her joy is that infectious.

"What brings you back to town so soon? You were just here, weren't you?"

I nod. "Life implosion."

I give her the quick-and-dirty version, leaving out the disturbing visuals. And that one awful second where I was actually excited that my fiancé was talking about marriage to me with his dangly parts still damp from another woman.

"Oh, my God," she says. "Did you knee him in the naked 'nads?"

"No," I admit. "But I probably should have."

"So are you moving back to Rush Creek?"

"No! No," I repeat, less vigorously, "I'm just visiting. And helping my mom with her new business."

"Ahhh," says Amanda. "I have heard her girls' night out parties are *hot*. Ask her if she'll do one for me and Lucy and Hanna—"

"What are you signing me up for?" Hanna demands, stepping out onto the porch. She's Kane's business partner and an honorary Wilder. Also, I wish I could pull off a pixie-cut the way she can—or that I was half as in shape. "Did I hear those accursed words, *girls' night out*?"

"You'll like this one," Amanda says. "*Promise*."

Hanna scowls, and Amanda starts to elaborate, but

Kieran gets bored with the rocking chair, dismounts chair and porch, and hurries back toward the backyard.

"I got him," Hanna says, and gives chase.

Amanda turns back to me and says something, but the growl of an engine drowns her out as a motorcycle takes the turn into the Wilder driveway a little too fast, kicking up wood chips and dust. It comes to a stop and Brody dismounts, removing his helmet and setting it down. The sun catches a glint in his hair, of course. He pushes his fingers through it, a habit he's had since childhood. His hair is always disheveled, which takes nothing away from it.

Ohhh, Brody Wilder, you are a work of art. A scowl-y, troubled, *troubling* work of art.

He's wearing bad-ass motorcycle boots, a form-fitting black t-shirt that shows off spectacular pecs and ripped abs, leather cuff bracelets on both wrists—one braided, one looped with chain—and a pair of ripped jeans.

As he gets closer, I try not to track each and every rip, but it's tough, and my eyes find the one at the top of his thigh, where the golden hair on his thick quads peeks through. My fingers itch to touch it. It's tough to look away.

I discover Amanda is watching me drool over Brody, amused. She raises her eyebrows at me, and I mouth, *Sorry*.

"No worries," she says. "I'm really fucking used to it."

It's possible I look alarmed, because she hastily adds, "I mean, not just him. All of them."

"Hey."

Brody utters the monosyllable in a honey-rich voice that I feel somewhere right below my belly button. Or, say, six inches lower.

I'm somewhat shocked to discover that he seems to be addressing me, or at least my general vicinity.

Brody Wilder doesn't talk much, and he never talks to me.

I got used to it during my long teen years when I pined for him and he seemed not to know I existed, except for the occasional, "Oh, hey, Rach," when he was at our house and I was impossible to ignore. Like, standing right in front of him.

"Oh, hey, Rach," Brody says, when he reaches Amanda's side, which I guess means he wasn't addressing me with the first "hey." Big surprise there.

"How are things?" I ask him, because making conversation is the polite thing to do in situations like this.

He shrugs.

Right.

I don't know if he hates me? Or just finds me so boring as to not be worth his time? Or...?

"Well," says Brody. "Guess I'll head into the backyard."

"I'm surprised you showed up," Amanda says. "Given that rumor has it Gabe's gunning for you."

Brody scowls. "He already laid into me. Figure I'm safe enough here with everyone around."

In response to my raised eyebrow, Amanda says, "The guys are trying to revamp their business to change with the times, and it's a better fit for some than others."

I'd heard a little bit about this plan from my mom and Connor. Just about the time the Rush Creek rodeo failed, a hot spring popped to the surface—apparently, hot springs naturally come and go on their own. The arrival of this one ushered in a whole lot of wedding-and-spa businesses. And the Wilders are trying to win over those tourists, because outdoor adventuring has taken a big hit recently.

Brody's permanent scowl deepens. "Book-club-on-a-boat," he says, darkly, to me. It's the most words he's said to me in a decade.

"Sounds fun?" I hazard, and the scowl settles into permanence. Yeah. He doesn't like me. I catalog the black-and-gray ink on his arms instead of sulking about his attitude. His tattoos are gorgeous, complex patterns—rain on a window, a school of interlocking fish, waves.

It must have taken someone hours to ink them—and it must have been a long, painful experience for Brody.

I bet he didn't even flinch.

Why is that so unbelievably hot to imagine? Brody, grim-faced and stoic under the needle.

Why, Rachel? Why are you having underpants feelings for a man who doesn't speak complete sentences to you?

Long, long habit.

Brody and Connor have been friends practically since birth, and I don't think I can actually remember the first time I realized I had an all-consuming, brain-melting crush on Brody.

What I do know is that Brody bought his first motorcycle while I was still in high school, which meant I got to watch him ride it in town, denim-clad thighs securely gripping it.

That fueled lots of fantasies, not that, in a million years, I ever would have indulged even one of them. If he'd shown up at my doorstep on that thing—assuming Connor didn't kill him first—I would have told him no thank you. Motorcycles are dangerous. I was too busy doing my schoolwork ahead of time and offering to help my parents with absolutely everything, strategies that let me carve out my own place, different from my brother's with his wild-child antics.

I was not too busy to lust after Brody though.

"You know what you should bring on the boat, Brody?" Amanda says. "Rachel's mom's girls' nights out. *That* would be a kick."

Brody's head snaps up and, wait, *this cannot be*, but *yes*, he is looking at me. Full-on blazing green eye contact for a fraction of a second. Then he looks away again, and thank God, because I was in danger of going up in flames like an ant caught in a magnified sunbeam.

"Yeah. Connor said something about that." He fidgets with an object in his hand. It looks like a miniature rabbit's foot, small, black, and fuzzy.

I feel a sudden blaze of sympathy for Brody, who has always struck me as desperately wanting to do right without knowing quite how to. I present as evidence the time it started to pour and he stopped his truck and gave me and my bike a ride home. And the time he bought me a new lunch after I dropped my tray in the cafeteria. And the time he drove me home from the one—literally only—party I have ever gotten drunk at, and didn't tell Connor or my parents.

He didn't say a word to me in any of those cases, except "You're welcome," when I said, "Thank you."

That's how I know that under that gruff, bad boy exterior, a kind heart beats.

I say, "Brody?"

He looks surprised that I've addressed him by name, but then, if our situations were reversed, I would be, too, right?

"Yeah?"

"If you'll forgive my assumption here," I say, "you don't seem like party-hosting is your jam."

He shakes his head.

"If you let us, my mom and I can take care of all of that. You just provide the venue."

I deeply hope this is true, and that my mother doesn't kill me later, but I remind myself that I'm mainly doing this for her, so she has no grounds for complaining. "If you're interested, let me or my mom know. I'm sure we can make it happen."

"I, uh, might be," he says.

Amanda makes a soft, choking sound.

"You okay?" I ask her.

"Swallowed wrong," she says, gesturing to her plastic cup of beer.

"Okay," I say. "I'll talk to my mom about it."

"I'll give you my phone number," Brody says, holding out his hand.

1) That was definitely a full sentence, and 2) He's asking for my phone. So he can enter his number in it.

My fourteen-year-old self squees so loudly and for so long that Brody says, impatiently, "Your phone."

I dig it out and hand it over, and he taps his digits in, then hands it back.

I'm doing this for Mom, I tell myself.

And Abuelita.

I am so full of it.

"Real Romance," I read off the side of the demo bin, as I set it down next to my mom. She's sitting in a comfy chair with her legs up on an ottoman in a Rush Creek living room, site of my first girls' night out. The women slowly filter from the kitchen—where the drinks and snacks are—into the living room. They arrange themselves in a circle, perched on kitchen chairs they hauled in.

"I thought it said 'Read Romance,'" I tell her. "Now that would be a great business, don't you think? Curated romance novels, sold direct, in the privacy of your own home party."

She looks like she's seriously thinking about it, so I say, "Kidding, Mami!" All the bins attended to, I position myself behind my mom, ready to bring her what she needs from her stash of boxes.

The women settle in, and my mom makes them all introduce themselves and explain why they accepted the RSVP.

The answers vary wildly. Quite a few women respond, "I was just curious!" A few say a friend made them come, shooting fond or dirty looks at the friend in question. Others use phrases like, "self care," "self-indulgence," or "luxury."

"I could use some new toys," one woman says, which seems like kind of an odd answer, but maybe she's one of those people who fully embraces a new hobby. Like, she'll buy the whole line of candles, or whatever, and the stands that go with them, and photograph them for Instagram, one per day, for thirty days....

Mrs. G—who also happens to have been my high school history teacher—says, "Not gonna lie. My vibrator is my best friend since my husband left three years ago." She makes a face. "Actually, it was my best friend for about a decade before that, too."

Record screech!

Her *vibrator*?

I look over at my mother, who is studiously not looking at me.

I look down at the bins.

Real Romance.

Personal care, my ass. Possibly literally.

"Mami," I say. "A word."

"Not right now, Rachel." She frowns.

I hold up a hand. "If you'll excuse us," I say to the circle of women.

My mother moves excruciatingly slowly on crutches, but finally we get far enough from the living room that I can whisper-yell, "What's in those bins?"

"Relationship enhancement," my mother says. "Intimacy aids."

"Sex toys?!"

"Shhh," she says.

"You're selling *sex toys!?*" And then, with dawning horror, "*We're* selling sex toys! On Brody's boat!"

Because my mom loved the idea of bringing her parties onto Brody's boat, and we agreed to do one tomorrow night.

Or, more exactly, I agreed to do one. My mom has already told me there's no way she can take the broken foot on a boat, and after watching how much she sucks on crutches, I had to agree with her. Tonight, I'm learning the script so I can fly solo tomorrow.

A truly, truly horrifying thought occurs to me.

"Oh, *God!*" I say. "Does Brody know what we're selling on his boat?"

"I think so?" my mom says.

"Not good enough!"

Pretty sure I yelled that, based on the fact that it suddenly got quiet in the other room.

She consults the ceiling, then says, "No, wait, yes. Yes. He definitely does."

I eye her suspiciously, but she says, "No, for sure. I gave him the website."

I'm honestly not sure if that's better or worse. Because now Brody Wilder thinks I offered to sell sex toys on his boat.

This is definitely not going to improve the Brody-hates-me problem.

"Rachel," my mother whispers. "We have to get back in there."

"You. Told. Me. Essential oils."

"I knew you wouldn't do it if I told you what it was."

"Damn straight!" I say.

"Rachel," says my mother. "I was dubious too. But please come back in that room with me. You'll see. I promise."

"I am not going back in there. My high school history teacher is in there. And my Spanish teacher!"

"I can't do it alone, Mamita. I can't. Look at me." She slumps on her crutches.

My mother does not employ the guilt trip too often, but when she does, she is an absolute, world-class expert.

"Please," she says. "At least stay for this. If you still hate it afterwards, you can bail. I will explain to Brody that you are afraid to handle the merchandise in his presence."

"I hate you," I whisper.

She smiles. "I know you don't."

We go back into the living room where our guests look at us curiously. Mrs. G, who definitely remembers me from high school, has clearly figured it out, because she tosses me a sympathetic look.

That's right, Mrs. G.

My wonderful but crafty mother kept me in the dark about the true nature of her business.

She starts demoing products, which means she tells me what to pull out of the bins and I do it.

At first, they are wholly non-threatening. Lotions, scented soaps, bath oils, hairbrushes. She segues into massage oil, and no one flinches. Next up is some kind of gel that makes you tingle wherever you rub it. I pass around the demo tube, and no one in the circle turns down the chance to rub a little on the back of their hand.

Oh, what the hell. When in Rome.

Ooh.

That's nice.

"You can use this on your clit or your labia, too," my mother says matter of factly.

Okay, pause.

I love my mom to death, but she was like most moms I knew, not a super-genius when it came to the teaching of sex ed. She did talk to me (briefly, blushingly) about the facts of life, and she supplemented with a couple of reasonably decent books that showed up on my bookshelf with no explanation whatsoever.

But I have never heard the words "clit" or "labia" out of my mom's mouth.

I kneel and pretend to be investigating something in one of the Real Romance inventory boxes to avoid showing my hot-pink face.

Would it be awkward if I went outside to "take a phone call?"

"The blue box, Rach," my mom calls, and I bring it to her and set it at her feet.

She starts pulling out actual toys—bullet vibes, eggs, and one she calls "the Cadillac of all vibrators" that looks like a garden-variety back massager. She hands them to me one by one. I'm supposed to distribute them around the circle. The women look like I feel, shellshocked, as I pass out the goodies.

Oh, God, I can't hack this.

The phone call idea is looking better and better.

And then, something happens. The women are reaching for the toys, powering them up, touching them to their palms and thighs. And talking.

"I've never used a vibrator," one says.

"You *have* to," another says.

"Do you use it by yourself?"

"Sometimes. Or with my husband."

"My husband's feelings would be hurt. He'd think it reflected on him."

"Let him use it on you," my mother says.

"Really?"

The other women jump in.

"Yeah, totally. Put on sexy lingerie and ask him to use it on you," says one.

"Give it to him for his birthday," says another.

The woman with the pink rabbit vibrator in her hands stares down at it, a smile creeping over her face.

I realize right then that my mother is a bit of a superstar.

"Can I say something?"

The speaker is one of the youngest women there. She hasn't been shy—she was one of the ones who said she was there because she was curious—but she hasn't been chatty, either. We all turn her way, and she says, "I haven't had an orgasm since I went on anti-depressants."

You know how everything turns on a dime at moments like that? It could go either way. Everyone in the room could fall awkwardly silent. Or...

The room is suddenly, chaotically abuzz.

"Me neither."

"Thank you so much for saying that."

"For me it's my blood pressure meds."

"After cancer, I couldn't get any satisfaction in the bedroom. And I miss it. I really miss it. Just, the intimacy. Is that weird?"

"No, hon. No. Not weird at all."

"Why does no one *talk* about this stuff?"

"Fucking menopause. It's like I'm numb from the waist down. And let's not even talk about the dryness thing."

"When I went on Prozac, I was like, *where were you all my life*? And then my sex life crashed and I was like, holy shit, I am not trading sex for happiness, and then one of my friends said, try this—" the speaker gestures to the Cadillac— "and then I realized, yes, you *can* have it all."

Needless to say, my mother's sales are brisk. And not just of the warming gel and lube. That Cadillac? Ten orders. One woman buys three. She says she's giving them to her sisters for Christmas this year.

That "ten orders" doesn't include mine. I can't get near the signup sheet, but I'm planning to place an order, too. Getting cheated on by your asshole boyfriend calls for a very special category of retail therapy, and it should definitely include a vibrator.

I'll add my order to the sheet in the car, right after I tell my mom that I totally, completely, and absolutely get why she loves what she's doing.

I t's a perfect night.

The sun is low and reflecting off the water. There's almost no breeze.

And Rachel Perez is a party whisperer.

I know she's a librarian, not a party planner, but I think this might be her other calling. She brought six bottles of wine, three shopping bags full of snacks, and an assortment of other things, including hand sanitizer.

I did manage to remember the bug wipes this time. I feel way too proud of myself. I'm also issuing toilet paper in five-square portions to each woman who asks to use the head. I've learned my lesson.

Rachel had the guests do introductions—I would never have thought of that—and now the women are sitting in the bow, chatting happily and passing around a small tube of hand lotion.

No small dogs are present.

Like I said, a perfect night.

Also, Rachel's wearing a pair of skin-tight jeans that show

off her amazing ass and a tank top that swerves over her perfect tits and makes my own jeans too tight.

I'm glad she's not wearing a sundress like the one she wore last Sunday to Gabe's housewarming. It had a scoop neck and thin straps that looked like they'd blow off her shoulders in a strong breeze. I tried so fucking hard not to stare down that neckline. And failed. So much soft skin, so much fodder for my late-night self-love.

I'm not sure what happened on that porch, to be honest. One minute I was sticking to my guns about what a bad idea it would be to have Rachel on my boat... and the next, I was giving her my phone number.

I blame the dress. And her mouth. And her Rachel-ness. The way her face got soft with sympathy right before she offered up her and her mom's services for the party. And something in me just caved, because I wanted her on my boat. Cheerful, beautiful, soft-hearted, kind Rachel. On. My. Boat.

Even if it's a terrible idea.

And now here we are. Me, still with my grave doubts, and her, with her swervy tank top. Every time a breeze kicks up, I look over to see if she's feeling the cold.

God help me.

"Okay, I was a little dubious about this until I tried it," Rachel says, holding up a sparkly gold tube.

I stop listening and just watch the sky, which is slowly turning an unearthly green-purple.

Until a few words catch my attention. In an unexpected and *very* visceral way.

"...on your clit or your labia..."

What the *fuck*?

I've just learned something. When a woman I'm hot for suddenly starts talking dirty out of the blue, my body reacts a split second before my brain. My dick is halfway to hard before my forebrain even comes online.

She's passing around more of those sparkly gold tubes, and I crane to see.

Sensual Heat.

Wait, *what*?

The women are laughing and exclaiming words of approval as they rub it on their hands and their faces.

I can't take my eyes off Rachel, who has smoothed a bit on her cheek to demonstrate. Fingertips sliding across her satin skin.

"Give it a second," she says, laughing. "It'll start to tingle."

The women are all oohing and ah-ing. Wanting to know how much it costs.

All I can think about is Rachel, tingling. Everywhere.

"Rachel," I hear myself saying. Sharply.

The women look up at the sound of my voice, and I wince.

She hurries back, ducking into the cockpit beside me.

"What is that?"

"Warming lube," she whispers, darting a look at her guests, who are watching us curiously.

I lower my voice, too. I don't want to ruin this party for her—or for me. The last thing I want is to reap another round of shitty reviews. "I mean, what's it doing here?"

She gives me a quizzical look. "I don't understand the question."

"I thought you were selling beauty products."

Her eyes get huge. Her mouth forms an O. And her hands spread open, like she's bracing herself.

"Rachel?" I murmur.

"You, um, didn't. You didn't, um, look at the website?"

Her cheeks have bright hot streaks across them. Something in my gut clenches in response to those streaks, like it would if I'd put them there.

I shake my head.

"Oh, God. God. Brody. I'm—I'm so sorry. My mom said she told you to look."

I vaguely recall this. And a text reminding me to check out the website that came in this morning from Mrs. Perez. *Just want to make sure you looked at the site so you know what you're getting yourself into.*

I just figured she meant that the products would all be floral scented and pink and that the participants would use the term "self-care"—one of Amanda's favorites—a lot.

I did *not* figure she meant that it would include lube. And—

Oh, shit.

"What else?" I demand.

My voice comes out gruffer than I mean it to, and she flinches. "Um," she says. She looks around a bit wildly, like someone might save her from this conversation. From me.

"Rachel," I warn.

"Toys," she whispers.

Connor is going to kill me. And not in a kind, efficient way. Slowly and with pleasure.

Wait. Connor. Does Connor know?

I review the contents of our conversation. What did he say?

Beauty stuff, like body wash and perfume and shit.

There was no wink-wink, nudge-nudge, and I cannot imagine Connor would deliver this blindsiding to me point blank.

Therefore, he must not know.

Oh, *shit.*

He cannot find out that Rachel is selling toys on my boat. He cannot.

But more to the point...

I look up, and there she is, tight tank top—and oh, hell, she's *definitely* cold—long, dark hair, and very worried expression on her face.

Rachel—Rachel who I have spent the last ten years of my life trying not to think about in a way that includes things like tingling, or lube, or *toys.*

Connor is a good friend, and I am not this good of a person.

Oh, fuck. Oh, *fuck.*

Also, God give me strength.

Rachel

A rush of humiliation washes over me, while I readjust to this new reality.

Brody did *not* know.

I just showed up on his boat and blindsided him with boxes full of sex toys.

I die.

Unfortunately, it's not that easy, and I am still standing

here on his boat, surrounded by curious onlookers, boxes of toys, and Brody, who looks as hot as always, and now—unsurprisingly—pissed.

"Do you want me to leave?" I whisper.

"Oh, God, no!" he whispers back. "Don't leave me alone with them!"

The desperation in his voice startles me—and makes me laugh. Which startles him. He turns his green gaze on me, and something in those eyes flares. Anger, I think.

"I'm sorry," I say quickly. "It's just—I wasn't planning to leave you with them. I assumed if I left they'd leave with me. But—I don't know, they did pay money to ride your boat, so maybe that was a faulty assumption."

Brody pulls something out of his pocket. It's that little mini rabbit's foot he fidgets with. He hides his gaze from me again, which is just as well because you're not supposed to stare into the sun that long.

"Look," he says, from under his bangs. "This wasn't what I expected... But please don't go. I, um, need this. I need to make this work. This business is what takes care of the whole Wilder family, and if I'm not pulling my weight..."

He trails off.

That was at least five sentences. A whole paragraph of Brody Wilder. The look on his face hurts my heart. Brody Wilder, veteran bad boy, wants desperately to do right by the people he loves, even if doesn't look like that's who he is from the outside.

"Of course I'll stay," I say.

The pained look softens into something much more like the Brody I'm used to. A scowl. "I'll just, I don't know, plug my ears." The corner of his mouth tips up, the scowl morphing into something more like a half-smile. I want to keep it.

"And close your eyes?" I murmur.

Unfortunately, the combination of the situation, the question, and my tone makes it sound super suggestive. The smile leaves his face and is replaced with something else, and humiliation swamps me again.

Ugh, as if it's not bad enough that I've just clobbered him with sex toys on his own boat, I'm flirting now. With a guy who has done everything he can to make it clear that I'm nothing more than his best friend's little, bitty, insignificant sister.

"I'll just..."

I gesture to the women, and practically run away from him.

"Everything OK?" someone asks me, as I rejoin them in the front of the boat.

"Yeah—just a little—misunderstanding."

I don't explain the nature of the misunderstanding, and no one asks. The women here tonight mostly didn't know each other before they showed up, and they're warming up a lot more slowly than the other group. Or maybe I don't have my mom's magic touch.

Speaking of magic touch, *oh, shit*, it's time for the vibrators.

I can't look Brody's way.

I won't look Brody's way.

Needless to say, the next few reveals are torture. I practiced a bunch so I wouldn't blush, but all my work is instantly undone. I blush my way through eggs, bullet vibes, remote control gadgets, straight up penis-clones, g-spot stimulators, shared vibrating toys. The women become fascinated, intrigued, confessional.

The rabbit.

The Cadillac.

Is he watching?

Is he scowling?

Half-smiling?

Or smirking?

Damn it, I have to peek.

Not watching. He's in the back of the boat. He has binoculars up and is staring at something on the shore.

"He's hot," says one of my guests.

"Really?" I say, like I hadn't noticed. "Yeah, guess so."

I look down into the box and realize that Jack Buddy's up next.

No.

My face is on fire.

I'm going to skip it.

Except...

According to my mother, Jack Buddy is a money-maker.

Anyone who pleasures a penis on a regular basis can appreciate Jack Buddy. Married straight women are mega fans. They like the idea that they can get their husbands off with a minimum of wrist damage and, on a bad night, without having to subject their soft parts to friction. Jack Buddy sold like hotcakes at the first party, and my mom confirmed that it's always a big winner.

No avoiding Jack Buddy, then. Because if I'm going to die of humiliation and have to avoid Brody for the rest of my life, I might as well make my mom some money.

"So," I explain. "This is Jack Buddy. Jack's a penile masturbation aid. Some people call them strokers."

I will not, will not, will not look at Brody. No matter how much it feels like my gaze is drawn to him by super magnets.

The women stare at the soft silicone sheath in my hand. They all have grabby-hand eyes, like they can't wait for me to get through my explanation so they can touch the foreign strangely-appealingly-pink-and-squishy sleeve.

Somehow—no idea how—I manage to get through my explanation and to pass the demo strokers around for the women to admire—and covet.

They're all discussing the marriage-saving possibilities.

"I mean, you could just lube it up and hand it over, right? When you have 'a headache'?"

"Or you could help out, if you were feeling generous."

"It would be kind of hot, watching, wouldn't it?"

It would be really, really hot, watching.

I glance at Brody again. I can't help it; my eyes won't obey my mind's command.

The binoculars are still in his hands. His eyes are still on the shore. But I can't help feeling like I have his attention, even so. Something in the set of his shoulders or the grip of his hands on the barrel of the binocs.

At the last minute, just as I'm about to look away, he turns.

It's only a split second, but I see those green eyes, filled with interest and heat.

And even though he turns back almost instantly, I'm sure of what I saw, because my body answers instinctively.

It's a heady feeling, and I'm afraid of how much I want more of it.

As the party winds down, Rachel tells the guests that if they leave a review for both Real Romance and Brody's Boat, they can also enter a special drawing, and she gives them a card with a QR code so they can find the drawing online and add their review links.

That's smart. I bet it'll help with the review situation.

Damn it. I don't need to feel absurdly grateful to her, on top of all my other complicated feelings.

Because obviously I'm going to tell her we can't keep doing this.

Otherwise, I'm going to keep thinking about things I shouldn't be thinking about. Like that goddamn Jack Buddy and whether Rachel thinks it would be hot to watch. Or all the places on Rachel the warming lube would make tingle. Or—

So many toys, so many possibilities.

I face-palm.

We pull into the marina, and the women hug Rachel, thanking her over and over again. Several of them program her number into their phones and tell her they want to grab drinks with her sometime. I can tell it surprises her, and I know from growing up around her that she was never the kind of girl who had a million friends.

Guess that's about to change.

Rachel is the last one to step out of the boat. Her hair, which is pulled back in a ponytail, ends in a soft, dark puff I desperately want to touch. She smells like flowers, I'm guessing from all the lotions and lubes she handled tonight. I hold out my hand to help her, and she takes it. I feel that touch everywhere on my body. Her hand is small but strong and warm, and her eyes meet mine as she steps onto the dock.

We're just a few inches from each other, and if I tugged on her hand, her mouth would pretty much fall onto mine.

"When will the order be ready?" a woman asks, breaking the spell.

"Ten days, give or take," Rachel says. "If you included your cell number, I'll text you when it's ready; otherwise, I'll email."

"Thank you!" the woman says, and melts away.

Rachel and I are alone. I search for the right words. Needless to say, I don't find them. Instead I say, "This is probably not a good idea."

"Oh," she says quietly, biting her lip. "Yeah. I get that."

"I mean, it's not you. You did—good. Like really good."

She looks at me, startled, like a compliment was the last thing she was expecting. Like, *who are you and what have you done with Brody?*

"I really appreciate the giveaway thing. That'll help a lot with reviews."

I notice she's doing it again. Getting that soft look on her face. I wish she wouldn't, because that's when I'm the most screwed. She can look hot for hours, but when she looks like *Rachel*, that's when I fall apart.

I'm trying not to think about all the Rachels she has ever been.

The one who used to bring Connor and me food in the treehouse, and looked like she was going to cry the one time I asked if she wanted to stay and eat some, too.

The one who used to make muffins and hand them around the neighborhood, while Connor and I modified our nerf guns to shoot nails.

The one who used to play "library" and "school" and "wedding" on the far side of the yard while Connor and I burned shit to the ground.

Even then she knew exactly what she wanted, and I knew she was going to get it. I also knew that no part of her plan included someone like me, who by age nine already excelled at pranks, destruction, and it's-better-to-ask-for-forgiveness-than-permission.

Rachel is still looking at me, soft and curious. And then she does a wonderful, terrible thing:

She licks her lips.

Just one quick swipe, tongue peeking out, the worst kind of tease.

It's all I can do not to lean forward and taste the spot she licked.

When my eyes leave her mouth and meet her eyes, she's watching me with her eyebrows up. And a smile tugging the corner of her mouth.

Rachel is no longer the teenager I spent years trying not

to want. She's all woman now, and I'm pretty sure her head is full of things I want to know about.

"Connor would kill me," I say.

Am I talking about sex toys on the boat? Or Rachel and me?

Doesn't matter; it's true either way.

The speculative look is still on her face, like she's wondering the same thing, but she nods. "Yeah. I'm sorry. I didn't find out till last night that that's what she was selling, and she told me you'd seen the website."

"I was supposed to. I just didn't. I'm not the best at following directions."

That makes her smile for real, which feels like a hundred thousand dollar win.

That's when I hear a truck pull into the parking lot several hundred feet away and look up to see Connor striding towards us, furious.

Oh, *shit*.

"Seriously? Neither of you thought to mention to me that Mom is selling vibrators? I had to find out from Jill at Oscar's?"

My breath whooshes out of me. Luckily, not as loud in reality as it feels in my chest.

"Oh, God, Con, I'm so sorry!" Rachel says. "I swear to God I didn't know you didn't know. I thought of course you knew, but it turns out Mom's quite the secret-keeper."

"Brody," Connor growls at me.

I hold both hands up. "Swear to God, Con, I was as in the dark as you. First I knew of it was when Rachel held up an eight-inch cock."

Rachel snickers at that. Million dollars.

"Are you telling me you just sold a bunch of women sex toys on your boat and you had no idea that's what you were inviting them here for?"

I've never been so relieved in my life to have been in the dark. "Swear it."

Connor takes a long look at my face. It's unnerving. It feels like he's trying to read my guilt on my face. And there's plenty of it, although not for deceiving him. For wanting his sister.

Just when I'm sure I'm going to blink first, he bursts out laughing.

"Holy shit," he says. "I would have loved to have seen your face."

I am so fucking thankful he didn't.

I'm LOCKING my truck in the parking lot of my apartment building when Connor pulls in. I wondered if he was going to chase me.

He hops out of his truck and heads my way.

I raise my eyebrows at him. "What's up?" As if I don't know.

"Look. As your friend. I'm asking. Don't do this."

I think about telling him to can it, but Connor is a good friend, and I don't want to do that. Besides, I've reached the same conclusion on my own. There is literally no way I can be on that boat with Rachel and her *merchandise* without losing my mind.

"I'm not," I say. "That was it. No more Booty-on-the-Boat."

"Catchy, though," he says almost regretfully. Then he pins

me with a look that makes me want to disappear. "My point is, she's off limits, Brody. She's trying to put her life back together. She keeps talking about getting it 'back on track.' She doesn't need to get distracted."

"Jesus, Connor. I know that. And also, you know that if she were here, she'd have a few things to say about how it's the twenty-first century and her brother is talking total bullshit."

He crosses his arms and glares, but he knows I'm right.

Still, I have to work hard not to feel like crap about this speech, about the part where she's *getting her shit back together* and I'm a *distraction*.

Connor, who has always had my back, is explicitly calling me off his sister because she's too damn good for me, and it stings.

Unfortunately, he's right about everything he said. Part of what I love about Connor is that despite the misguided shit we did as teenagers, he's a decent guy. What he said the other day about Rachel makes total sense. If she just got dumped, she's probably on the rebound. Rebounds make you reckless, make you do stuff out of character. I could totally see a life-long good girl like Rachel deciding now would be the perfect time to get herself some bad boy dick.

And that would be the shittiest reason in the world for me to blow up my friendship with Connor and risk hurting Rachel.

Not to mention, I don't want to be Rachel's bad boy dick.

"I won't touch her," I promise.

Connor's shoulders fall with so much relief that my stomach plummets again.

He really, really doesn't want me with his sister.

I know I shouldn't be surprised by it—I'm no one's prize —but it still hurts.

Connor sees me wince. "Hey, man. Look. This is for you, too. You're not in a good place to deal with any woman's rebound shenanigans. Zoë wrecked you. This thing with Justin—" He nods. "It would fuck up any guy with a heart. Just—give yourself a break and don't do anything half-assed till you have some time to sort yourself out."

He's right, he's right, I know he's right.

But I can still see her, standing on my boat, clutching Jack Buddy in one hand, peeking over to see if I'm paying attention.

I am, Rachel, I am.

8

Several days after sex-on-a-boat, I have to go into the office to grab some paperwork. Not coincidentally, it's lunchtime, which is the best time to show up at Wilder Adventure headquarters, because Amanda, who is a great cook, brings us lunch from her catering business.

I pull into the parking lot on my bike, remove my helmet, and sit there for a moment trying to get my head screwed on straight. I've been doing a lot of this—and also a lot of jerking off late at night—since that party.

My phone buzzes and I lunge for it. I've been doing that a lot, too, even though there's no reason Rachel would call me, and many reasons she wouldn't.

But this time it *is* actually her.

"Hey," she says.

"Hey."

She takes a deep breath, which she does when she has to do something that scares her—like the time Connor and I dared her to jump out of the treehouse.

Side note: She did it, and sprained her ankle, and Con and I got grounded for weeks.

"So. I know you said sex toys on the boat was a bad idea, and I totally get it. But my mom said it was one of her best selling-nights, and she really wants us to do it again." She hesitates. "She's trying to make enough money to bring my abuelita to Rush Creek."

Rachel has two grandmothers, but only one gets to be *abuelita*. I get a strong flash of her, a small, soft woman with a big, strong hug.

"I love your grandmother," I say, surprising myself.

"Oh," she says softly. "Yeah. I almost forgot you spent a lot of time around her."

"I want to help, but—"

But I can see Rachel standing in the boat with her small fingers around an eight-inch silicone cock and I can hear Connor saying, *Don't do anything half-assed till you have some time to sort yourself out.*

"Don't feel like you have to answer right away," Rachel says. "Think about it. Text me later."

"Okay," I say, and hang up, feeling...

Way off balance.

A car pulls into the parking lot next to my bike, and Lucy, Gabe's girlfriend and Wilder's savior, hops out. "Hey, Brody!" she calls.

I pocket my phone and follow her. We stroll toward the Wilder offices, which are in a big, revamped barn building. It was originally part of a ranch, but before I was born, the ranch was sold off and turned into housing parcels. Our family home, where I grew up, was one of the houses that got built here. There was a barn on the land, too, which my dad made them leave up, because he knew it would be the perfect new headquarters for Wilder Adventures, which he'd inherited from his own dad. He and my brothers and I gutted the barn and built the new Wilder together.

I loved that, when we were all working on the barn together.

"How's the boat biz going?" Lucy asks.

I know she's asking because she's friendly and supportive, but my hackles still go up a little, because fundamentally, she's on Gabe's side. I wonder if she's seen the reviews. If she knows about the ultimatum. "Fine," I say, and shrug.

I hadn't mentioned to either her or Gabe beforehand that I was doing a girls' night party with Rachel, figuring if it was a miserable failure, there'd be no need to bring it up, and if it was a success, there'd be plenty of time to brag.

It was a success, but at the moment, I'm too confused to feel triumphant. Plus I'm not sure how to bring it up.

I accidentally sold some sex toys in the Wilder name the other night feels like a lit firecracker.

Suppressing a sigh, I hold the door open for Lucy, and she steps into the barn.

There are offices at the far end of the room and a big conference table in the middle, with loads of equipment on shelves and racks and in bins around the perimeter.

I loved headquarters as a little kid. It felt loaded with possibility. You could grab an armful of stuff and head out into the woods, or onto a lake, a river, a ski slope. You could have any adventure you could imagine.

That said, since my dad died, headquarters isn't my favorite place. For one thing, it reminds me of losing him—and of the pain of his choosing Gabe over me to run Wilder. I

mean, not that I thought he'd give Wilder to me and not Gabe
—but it hurt like hell when he didn't ask us to run it together.
Or even give me a hint that he wanted me to be Gabe's partner. We were barely a year apart in age, but it had been clear
for a while at that point that Gabe was the chosen one and
I was...

Well, I was the screwup.

Welcome to my inheritance, which is feeling like the
brother who didn't make the cut.

"Are you working at Wilder this afternoon?" I ask Lucy, to
distract myself from all the history and my dark thoughts.

She shakes her head. "Just mooching lunch."

Lucy spends some afternoons at Wilder, because even
though she runs her own marketing company from an office
over Rush Creek Bakery in town, we're one of her biggest
clients.

And I'm sure the fact that Gabe's here is a plus. Not to
mention that Gabe's house is just over yonder, and sometimes
they both disappear for twenty minutes in the middle of the
work day.

Lucy, who has taken a few steps away from me, suddenly
turns back, phone in hand. "By the way," she says, holding up
her phone. "You're a hit!" She hands it to me so I can see. It's
my Brody's Boat page, and there are eight new reviews, one
from each woman on the boat the other night. They're all
five-star, and they're all glowing.

*Wish high school sex ed had been this matter-of-fact and plea-
sure-oriented.*

Best hours I've ever spent on a boat.

A great time in a gorgeous setting.

Every woman should take a ride on Brody's Boat.

"Gabe, check it out!" Lucy says, before I can stop her.

Lit firecracker. Alert!

Like some kind of turret gun, Gabe's attention, which had been on Easton, swivels to me. He strides across the room and, when I refuse to hand him Lucy's phone because *lit fire-cracker*, takes out his own and starts scrolling.

Lucy is ecstatic. "There are so many amazing lines from here we can use!" she says. "I'm going to do a whole campaign around this. Seriously. How many of these parties can Rachel do? Find out. Really. We can fill them all." She smiles at me. "You're a super genius!"

I realize that Lucy knew what Rachel was selling. Lucy knew, which means Amanda knew, which means she stood there and let me have that conversation with Rachel at Gabe's party and didn't try to stop me.

I'm going to kill her.

"It was Connor's idea," I say, because I hate taking credit for other people's shit. "And Amanda's, too, I guess."

"I appreciate your shout out," Lucy says, "but you still get to take credit for recognizing a brilliant idea when someone brings it to you. You're the business owner."

Lucy has a way of making everyone feel great about what they're doing, which is one of the many reasons it's impossible not to love her, despite the havoc she's wreaked. Plus, obviously, she's a great complement to Gabe, since heaping praise on us is not one of his strong points.

I start to say I didn't know the merchandise was sex toys when I agreed to host the parties, but I decide to shut the fuck up. After all, I did agree to let Rachel and her mom sell stuff I knew women loved. So maybe Lucy's right. Maybe I deserve some of the credit.

If we're giving credit, that is, which I'm pretty sure Gabe won't be doing. Sure enough, when I look up, Gabe has an eyebrow raised. "Sex toys, huh?"

"Yeah," I say, in a *you-want-to-make-something-of-it?* tone.

"Congratulations on the good reviews."

I know him too well to get excited about the compliment. Plus, he's still frowning.

"But a few good reviews are not a business model."

And here we go.

"I have a lot of questions."

"I'm sure you do," I mutter.

"Is this sustainable? Can you keep bringing in attendees, or will the market get saturated? What if Rachel or her mother decide parties on boats don't work for their business, then what? Can you convert these customers into ones who'll pay for other experiences?"

"Gabe," Lucy says.

"You know these are real questions," he tells her, in a way gentler tone. "Along with, will there be some customers who don't like the fact that we're peddling sex toys?"

That gets my blood up. "They can go fuck themselves. What Rachel's doing is great. Yeah, she's selling sexy stuff, but she's also educating. You should have seen those women. They had fun, and they learned a lot, too. If we have customers who are uptight about this, they can fuck right off."

Gabe draws back, obviously startled by my speech—and my vehemence.

But he doesn't argue. He looks at me, considering, and then nods. "I need numbers," he says. "Show me the numbers."

And once again I'm staring at his back as he strides away.
Damn it.

This is such a familiar scenario. The way my stomach clenches, I might as well still be the teenager who just lost his first job after showing up late for the third time in a row.

Nothing I do will ever be good enough for Gabe.

Lucy's face is sympathetic. Her kindness makes me feel, if anything, a tiny bit worse than Gabe's hardassery.

"You got this, Brody," she says. "We're going to make this work. I'm going to go get started on your campaign. Line up as many of these as you can with Rachel and let me know the dates."

"Thanks." I hand her back her phone, which she pockets before heading back to her workstation.

I pull out my own phone and take another look at the reviews.

It was fun to talk about this stuff.

What a great setting for a party.

I'm pissed at Gabe, sure.

But for a change, that familiar emotion is warring with an unfamiliar one. It's definitely quiet, muted—but it's there.

Pride.

And that's the emotion that makes me text Rachel:

Let's do it.

"Louisa," I plead over the phone. "I need your help."

Louisa is a first-class bestie. After I saw Werner's butt, Louisa helped me pack up my stuff and get the hell out of that apartment. I slept at her place that night, and we shuttled the rest of my stuff into storage and found me a plane ticket. Meanwhile, she pushed boxes of tissues, glasses of water, chocolate, and wine at me, listened as I told the story of where *perfect* had landed me, and instructed me that I should have a rebound fling with "that bad boy."

Ages ago, I'd mentioned that Brody was my first crush. Unrequited. She wanted to know if I'd ever tried to see if it could be requited, and I said that Brody had never given me even the slightest sign that he was interested in my existence, let alone my lady bits.

Anyway, I told Louisa, by the time I'd had the wherewithal to stage anything like a seduction, Connor had gone off to college and Brody had stopped coming around. She said that was lame, and I said it was life.

We were probably both right.

"You got it! What's up?" she asks me now, in response to my SOS.

"I need to bag the bad boy."

She screams on the other end of the phone, and I have to pull it away from my ear. When it's safe to resume holding it by my head, she says, "Rachel Perez, are you going to do something that's not in the plan?! Say it isn't so!"

Louisa and I are opposites-attract friends. She has never had a plan in her life, and I have rarely moved a muscle without one. It works, somehow, the way these things do. But we make fun of each other a lot, which is probably how we cope with how impatient we make each other. Like, Louisa is basically never on time. *Ever.* And I pretty much won't say yes to anything if I don't have twenty-four hours to plan it.

"You have to tell me everything. *Everything!*"

"It's a long, zany story."

"I've got time."

It's hard to know where to start, but I tell her about my mom breaking her foot and about the first girls' night out.

"Wait, *what?*" Louisa demands. "You? You're selling *sex toys?* How does that even *happen?* Was *that* in the plan?"

"No," I say. "It was definitely not in the plan. But I kind of love it."

I tell her about the parties I've done. How the women talk to each other, the confessions they make, and the healing they do.

"That's really cool. But what does this have to do with the bad boy?"

"I told you it was a long story. The bad boy?"

"Yesssss?"

"He has a boat."

"Okaaayy?"

"And, long story, but the gist is, his family owns an outdoor adventure business—you know, it's the Pacific Northwest—and they're trying to get more business from spa-and-wedding tourists, and he asked me to do a girls' night out on his boat."

"And you said *yes*?" she demands. "To selling sex toys on his boat?"

I can't exactly claim credit for that decision. I explain about how I didn't know it was sex toys. And neither did Brody.

"But then I found out and I did it anyway."

I tell her about the women at my first party and how they inspired me with their bruised but brave sex lives and their honesty.

"Holy shit, Rush Creek Rachel is incredibly badass."

She kind of is, I think.

"Yeah, well, she needs to be even more bad...tushy." Gopher butt, I'm talking about myself in the third person. "*I* need to be even more badtushy. I need to seduce him."

I could swear Louisa is cheering.

I start to explain about Jack Buddy and she jumps in. "Oh, my God, I used to love that thing when I was dating this guy who was totally obsessed with hand jobs!"

I tell her about Brody's studied disinterest, and, most importantly, what happened after the party. How Brody was staring at my mouth, how he looked up guiltily and said, "Connor would kill me," and how we both knew he didn't mean for selling vibrating bunnies on his boat. And I update her on the state of the union with the parties, that after he said he didn't want to do any more, he agreed to do at least a second one, in a few days.

"So? So? What are you going to do about it?"

"Well," I say. "I don't know. It's confusing. He *is* my brother's best friend. This could be the small town equivalent of a diplomatic incident. Maybe even declaration-of-war level."

"Rachel," she says sternly. "You are *not* going to miss your chance to bag the bad boy because your big brother might get testy with you."

"No," I agree. "That would be criminal."

"So? What's the plan?"

"I guess... I'm going to seduce Brody Wilder, on his boat, with a sparkly purple dildo?"

She giggles. "It sounds like a kinky game of Clue. I guess now we know what the rope and the candle were really for."

"Candlestick."

I can practically hear her rolling her eyes. "*Candle.* Like, wax. You know."

"Wax?"

"Oh, Rachel," she groans. "You have so, so much fun ahead of you."

"I need a strategy," I say.

"Do you?" she asks. "It sounds like you're doing pretty well without a plan."

I picture the smolder in Brody's green eyes and decide she's right. Also, for the first time in my life *without a plan* sounds strangely wonderful.

"Oh, shit!" Louisa cuts into my fantasy, sounding panicked. "I just realized I'm supposed to be on a work call as of three minutes ago. Gotta run. Enjoy your walk on the wild side!"

"My walk on the Wilder side," I correct, giddy. "It's way wilder than picking your scarf with your eyes closed, right?"

That's one of the things Louisa makes fun of me for, that I have fifty-five days worth of interchangeable work clothes (eleven shirts, five pants; can be worn in any combo), but I choose my scarves daily with my eyes closed, to shake things up.

Louisa snorts. "Fuck yeah. Have fun, girl!"

We say goodbye, and I swipe to hang up.

"Who was that?" a deep voice behind me asks from the doorway, and I nearly jump out of my skin.

"Connor! I didn't know you were here! Where's your truck?"

And, oh, megadooky! Was he listening?

"Dad took it to Home Depot. I was helping Mom with some stuff. Sorry, didn't mean to startle you."

Nah. He couldn't have been listening, because he doesn't look particularly concerned. And I know Connor doesn't hold back when he has an opinion, which he definitely would if he'd heard anything I'd said about Brody.

Connor is intensely protective of me, and always has been. One of my most cherished memories is of the time when Connor was teaching me to ride a bike. He kept saying, "I won't let you fall, Rachey!" Finally my dad came outside and made Connor let him take over. It took me all of five minutes after that to ride on my own. When Connor grumped about my dad taking all the credit for his hard work, my dad told Connor: "You can't teach someone to ride a bike if you won't let her fall."

Yep. That's Connor.

The universe must be looking out for me, because a

moment later, my dad pulls up and climbs out of the truck, and Connor gives me an unconcerned wave, jumps in, and drives away.

Whew.

If I'm going to walk on the Wilder side, I should probably do it a little more stealthily.

The night after Lucy spots my good reviews, Kane and Hanna corner me in the office after work and invite me to Oscar's Saloon & Grill with them.

I've mostly stayed away from Oscar's since the incident where I got stinking drunk and picked a (well-deserved) fight with Len Dix, but Kane is insistent.

"Brody." Kane is my most level-headed brother. "You can't stay away from Oscar's forever. It has the best burgers in town."

"Wait, you're going to Oscar's?" Easton demands, appearing out of nowhere. He has a way of doing that when there's the slightest opportunity for a night out, a party, or getting laid.

"Right," Hanna says. "I just remembered I have to wash my hair tonight."

"Go easy on me, Han," Easton says. "I've been a good boy lately."

"Meaning you spent at least one night in your own bed this week?"

Hanna and Easton have been frenemies as long as any of us can remember. They were in the same class at school, and when Hanna applied for employment at Wilder Adventures, Easton begged Gabe not to hire her. "She *hates* me," he pleaded, but Gabe said Hanna was too good at what she did to let that get in the way. He'd said she'd be mostly working with Kane, and Easton wouldn't see her that often.

That didn't turn out to be true, but somehow Easton and Hanna have tolerated each other all these years.

And they're very good entertainment.

There must be some kind of magnetic field whenever three or more Wilder brothers are gathered, because Gabe and Clark drift over, then, shortly after that, Amanda. Before I can come up with a good excuse, I'm being shepherded into Gabe's Jeep and driven into town.

And to be honest, it's really nice. I've been in a weirdly good mood all week, ever since the reviews came out, and for a change, I don't feel like there's a wall of black fog between me and Gabe. The seven of us cram into a booth made for six, and we drink and kid around. Even Clark jokes a bit, showing more life than he has in months. Then people start drifting away, until it's just Kane, Clark, Easton, and me, and the conversation turns to the whole Wilder Adventures revamp. Kane's starting to plan a big winter holiday event to fundraise for breast cancer survivor support—the Tinsel and Tatas Winter Games & Gala. Clark's got some fancy RVs in the works, but short term, he, Gabe, and Lucy are hosting glamped-up camping trips with—"Get this," he says, rolling his eyes. "Shower tents and toilet tents."

"Wait, so—someone has to hump that?" Easton asks.

"Yeah, that's why I'm bringing backups."

"No," Kane protests. "That's gotta be twenty pounds, at least."

"Yup. Making Gabe carry it."

We all laugh.

All of a sudden Kane, who's facing the back of the restaurant, gets a look on his face. Alarm bells go off in my mind. "What?"

"Nothing." But he gets up from where he's sitting—on the other side of the booth with Clark—and slides in next to me. Which is fucking weird. I turn around to look, and *shit*.

It's Zoë, with a sleeping Justin in her arms, and Len Dix, and they're coming toward our booth.

Now I get why Kane changed seats. To hem me in so I couldn't get up. That's Kane for you: the peacemaker, the problem-solver, the trouble-soother. When we were kids and the rest of us were beating the shit out of each other, Kane was mediating, making us "use our words" and "talk it out."

I have to admit, I can't help wondering if Kane actually likes running trips. All us other Wilder brothers are living our best lives—well, except for our romantic disasters—but Kane? I don't know. Sometimes I think he might be happier doing something else.

"Hi, Brody," Zoë says. Her brown hair is pulled back in a too-tight ponytail, her skin is paler than usual, and there are dark circles under her eyes. "Hey. Kane, Clark, Easton."

My brothers all give her tight unsmiling nods.

Love them.

Len Dix doesn't say anything, and he doesn't make eye contact. He's a big white guy. Beefy and bearded. He looks like a lumberjack, and for good reason—he runs his dad's lumbermill, employing an army of axe-wielding bearded dudes.

"Hi, Zoë," I say. "Little late for Justin to be out, right?"

Well, shit. Didn't know I was going to say it until it was too late.

"Not your concern, Wilder," Len says.

I don't have time to make a decision before I realize I'm being wrestled back into the booth by Easton and Kane, while Clark says, "Move along, Zoë—that's what you're good at, anyway, right?" Through the red haze of my rage I see Len start to round on my brother, but Clark gets to his feet and Len seems to think better of it. Clark's as big as Len, and even a dumb Dix wouldn't take on four Wilders in the middle of Oscar's.

Then they're gone and the fight fizzles out of me.

Easton pushes his half-full glass of whiskey across the table and I down it.

"Thanks," I say.

I mean, *Thanks for the whiskey,* but also, *Thanks for not letting me kick the shit out of him. Thanks for having my back. Thanks for knowing the right thing to say and the right thing to do, even though I haven't been able to tell you what the fuck's going on.*

"Of course," Easton says, and Clark and Kane nod. Not the tight one. The one that says, *We're brothers.*

Which is sometimes all you need to know about us.

I wonder what would have happened if they hadn't been here.

And for some reason, right then, I think about Rachel. Maybe it's because she was there the last time I hit Len. Maybe it's because most nights I haven't been able to get her out of my head since she brought all those wiggly, vibrating objects onto my boat. Maybe it's because right about now, Connor's words are coming back to me:

Just don't do anything half-assed till you have some time to sort yourself out.

Amen to that, friend.

RACHEL

By the time I do Brody's second party, I've hosted a couple more with my mom and have a pretty decent sense of the rhythm and flow. It's basically like good sex: lots of conversation, plenty of foreplay, and then the lube comes out.

"So this—" I hold it up and take a quick peek to see where Brody is. He's just outside the cabin door, standing and studying the sky, which is ribbed with wispy clouds.

He's wearing his usual: jeans that on anyone else would be next week's trash, but are living their best life cupping his business. Of course, boots—badass boots—do women get to ask men to leave their boots on in bed? I'm seriously considering it. Assuming I can get him into bed...

"This is warming gel. There are so many fun things you can do with it." I planned ahead for this. Yes, planned. I wasn't planning to plan. It just happened. I pour a tiny bit of gel into a bunch of those little paper cups you get free samples in at the grocery store and pass them around. "You can rub it in almost anywhere, and it'll warm up and start to tingle. Lips, clit, nipples, labia..."

I practiced that about a thousand times in the mirror earlier, and I manage the whole explanation without stuttering even a little. Which is good, because when I sneak a glance his way, Brody has quit staring at the sky and is watching me. Green-eyed and intent. Yes.

"Try dabbing a little on your lips."

I dip a fingertip into the paper cup and run it over my lower lip. The women follow suit.

"Oh, wow!"

"That's amazing."

"Oh, yeah, I can see how that would work other places, too."

"It's edible," I inform them, licking it off my finger and taking a quick peek Brody's way. His eyes are fixed on my mouth. On the finger between my lips. My body warms like someone has slicked the gel between my legs. Brody leans his head against the cabin door, eyes never leaving my face. The heat in my sex thickens and twists.

Auria, one of the women at my party, notices Brody and calls to him. "You want some, Brody?" She and her wife Tilly are both here. Auria owns Spa Day Sandwiches and Tilly owns Glory Day Spa.

Brody scowls. "No, thanks."

"Works for men, too!" I say cheerfully.

He narrows his eyes at me. I bite back a smile.

"What would happen if you put it on his balls?" one of the women whispers, mostly to herself. I know she doesn't, literally, mean Brody's but I get an immediate and vivid mental picture.

"I don't know." I hesitate. "But you could buy some and try it." *Not on Brody*, I add, silently, riding an unexpected wave of possessiveness.

We move on to the little rubber clit stimulator—always a crowd pleaser—then the ben wa balls. And I get a dropping sensation in the pit of my stomach. I'm about to do something outrageous, definitely nothing like picking a random scarf out of the drawer.

"So these—" I hold up the ben wa balls. "—are for strengthening your Kegel muscles, and also, if you leave them in, the effort to hold them in place can be very pleasurable. And they're incredibly discreet. I could have two in right now, and you'd never know it." I shrug. "I might."

I wait a beat. Two beats. Three. Then I check. Just to see.

His eyes are a thousand degrees of heat. They're burning through me. I'm going to go up in flames. My inner muscles clench around the (non-existent) ben wa balls.

I should've followed my impulse before the party. I'd thought about it a long time, holding an unopened box in my palm. I'd even taken them out—committing myself to the purchase—balancing their heavy, tantalizing weight in my palm. And then I'd chickened out of inserting them.

I pass the demo balls around.

"I've never been a balls girl," one of the partiers says, both speculatively and impishly. "But these could change my mind."

Snickers.

"Yeah, but it would be awkward if yours were bigger than his," another guest says.

I look up and discover Brody smirking at me. He shakes his head.

My chest wings open like a bird taking off. It's the smirk. Scowling Brody, I can deal with. Smirking, not so much.

Fight fire with fire, I think, and meet his amused eyes with a tease in my own. His expression changes—dark lust now.

I go hot all over, in waves.

"What's next?" a partier demands, yanking me back to my task. Every group is different, I'm finding. These women are ready to roll with the harder-core toys when I bring them out. In general, they've been a rowdy crew, demolishing wine at an alarming speed. They're almost all divorced, no-nonsense, and no-holds-barred.

Brody leans back against the edge of the cabin door, watching. Crosses his arms. His gaze is on me now. I don't have to speculate about where his attention is—it's fully mine. And the intensity of it, of that green-eyed fire, streaks hot through me, like the ghost flickers that sparklers leave behind.

The vibrators are causing so much joy in this crowd. This is a group that'll turn every last one on, teasing their fingertips and their thighs before handing them back. I pass a thumb over the head of something hot pink and pleasingly smooth, then look up to find Brody with his eyes so languorously heavy that I almost drop the toy. Lashes practically touching his cheeks.

The buzzing toy in my hand doesn't look like a real penis, but I wonder what those eyes would do if I slicked my thumb over his.

I raise my eyebrows at him, asking, and he narrows his eyes at me, mock anger, but I know he's not really mad, because a corner of his mouth curls up.

THE PARTY GOES from rowdy to rowdier. The stories they're sharing are hilarious and hair-raising. Rush Creek is small enough that the divorced population is pretty incestuous. Apparently, it's not uncommon to sleep with the parent of one of your kids' friends. Or your kid's pediatrician. Teacher. Basketball coach.

"Wait, basketball coach?" one of the women, Amy Pearson, asks. She has thick red hair, lots of freckles, and a curvy body shown to its best advantage by a great pair of jeans and a scoop necked top.

They're all still laughing except her.

Then Cara Yun—dark-haired, slender, wearing a calico wrap-dress—says his name. He's young, mid-twenties, and new as of last year, so I don't remember him from high school. Apparently he's also hard-bodied, raring to go 24/7, and enthusiastic about her pleasure. She's having multiple orgasms for the first time in her life. "Benton's the first guy who's willing to put in the work."

Amy's gone pale. "Wait," she says again. My heartrate ticks up. "Benton? Like Benton Frusk?"

Cara nods.

"You're sleeping with Ben?"

"Wait, *you're* sleeping with Ben?"

Things go off the rails then, Amy and Cara both on their feet, yelling, each saying they'd seen him first, that the other *knew* she liked him.

The other women are dead quiet for at least five seconds, then some dive in, some take sides, some try to soothe their yelling friends. I'm on my feet and calling for order. I'm hoping to return the group to their party spirit and open wallets, but tantrumming toddlers have nothing on this group, and as the fray escalates, the boat literally starts rocking.

"Enough." The voice is deep, decisive, and calm.

Brody has stepped into the bow, into the middle of our group, where he stands with his arms crossed, which makes his forearms and biceps bulge. His ink flares, and so does something between my legs.

"Take your differences elsewhere. This is a party."

Our clients have gone silent. I'm apparently not the only one impressed by Brody's ability to take charge. They're all staring at him, rapt, Benton Frusk temporarily forgotten.

Brody turns and goes back to the helm, depriving me of the view. The party feels like it must be over, and this isn't the closing ceremony I'd hoped for. I'm aware I have about five seconds to rescue it. Not enough time to think. I have to improvise.

Luckily, I have some recent experience with worthless men like this two-timing coach, and there's one super important thing I know about them.

They don't deserve the women they mess with.

"Amy," I say. "Cara."

They both turn to look at me.

"He's not worth it."

I'm saying it about Benton Frusk, but I'm thinking it about Werner.

"He would be lucky to have either of you."

I'm not just saying this to make them feel better. I like them both. I just met them tonight, but you'd be surprised how much of a feel you can get for someone by talking about sex with her for an hour-plus. Sex isn't just sex, as I'm discovering. It's wrapped up with everything. Childhood issues, current illness. Your self esteem, your friendships. Frustration. Loss. Hope.

It's wrapped up with being human and being fragile and being strong.

So I feel like I know a little bit about Amy and Cara, just from watching them drink wine and support their friends and lose their stuff.

I cross my arms. "And if he doesn't know that he'd be lucky to have either of you, then he definitely doesn't deserve both of you."

They both stare at me. Then, warily, they look at each other.

"Amy?" Cara asks.

"Mmm-hmm?" Amy says.

"Want to make Benton Frusk regret some life decisions?"

A smile creeps over Amy's face, and the two women shake on it.

In the relative quiet, I bring out the order forms—clearly I'm not going to sell any more product after *that*—and Brody pilots the boat back to the marina.

"Whew," he says, when they're all gone.

We're standing on the dock, catching our breath, coming down from the intensity of the party. It's dusk now, the sun's dipped below the horizon, the sky is starting to darken. He's close to me, the warmth streaming off his body, his leather and musk scent. I'm hyper aware of him. I've spent the last hour talking about sex, handling model penises, and watching Brody look at me like he wants to devour me. It's enough to make a girl buy stock in panties.

"Is that going to happen a lot?"

I shake my head. "Pretty sure Benton Frusk is going to be more careful about his multi-tasking after the two of them are done with him."

"That was cool." He ducks his head, not quite looking at me. "What you said to them. You can think on your feet. I wish I could."

"You did," I say.

"Yeah, but I was all brawn. You were finesse."

I laugh at that. "I'm flattered, but—I think it was more desperation than finesse."

"Well, you're good at that. Keeping things from blowing up. Keeping the party on track."

"Thanks." I duck my head.

"And the other thing, too. Explaining the products. Selling them."

I lift my chin and meet his gaze, green and hungry. He's staring at me. Not looking away. It's almost too much. I have the ridiculous thought that Brody limits his eye contact because it's a controlled substance. And he doesn't talk because he doesn't need to. His body is eloquent. Green eyes, the tilt of his head, the tension in his shoulders, his clenched fists.

All that tension sets up an answering coil of heat in my body.

"There's something I need to know." His voice has dropped, low and husky.

"What's that?" My own voice is barely audible.

"Do you?"

I don't know what he's asking, but I feel like he's cast a spell over me. I can't move. I'm just—waiting. For what's already happening. Whatever he wants to know, the question is heavy with intent.

"Do I what?" I dare.

"Have two in right now?"

I'm still puzzled.

He holds his hand out. My gaze drops to it. He rolls two invisible, imaginary ben wa balls in his palm, and the sparklers in my body give way to fireworks.

I make a small helpless sound, and his pupils flare, wide

and needy.

"Brody—"

His voice is rough. "Because it's all I can think about."

I shake my head. "No. But—you're making me wish I did."

It's his turn to utter a dark, wordless groan. Because we both know what I mean. That I need to be full. Filled.

I'm breathless. I can feel the slick of my body's lube on the swollen lips of my sex.

He catches me as my knees sag, tugs me into his arms, and kisses me with a rough desperate sound. His hands cup my head, his mouth opens and slants over mine, and I can't breathe or think. I clutch his head, his hair, his shoulders. His thigh slides between mine, and I can't help myself, I move against it, hungry and helpless.

And then as fast as it started, like a summer thunderstorm, it's over, and he steps back. I'm left panting, revved up, needy. I want to grab him and hold him—but I don't.

"I—" Brody attempts. For a split second I'm sure he's going to apologize and I will have to disembowel him, but he shakes his head. "Wow, Rachel."

My voice is shaky. "Can we do that again?"

He laughs, a honey-rough, perfect sound. Then he sobers, the rare and beautiful smile falling away. "Can we talk a minute first?"

I raise my eyebrows. "That's not your line."

"I know. But I don't think on my feet, like I said."

Part of me doesn't want to talk. It just wants to *do*, to keep kissing and touching.

To be filled.

But it's starting to rain now, just a few droplets, and if our situations were reversed, I know I'd want him to hear me out. Not rush me.

I say, "Maybe in the truck?"

We climb up. He sets both his hands on the steering wheel, but doesn't start the engine. He just sits there. The silence rolls out between us. The windows are down. I can hear us breathing, even above the shrill sound of tree frogs and crickets.

"I know this whole thing is weird. Me being your brother's friend, and all."

"Yeah. It is."

"And you're selling sex toys on my boat."

"Relationship enhancement products," I say, reflexively, which makes me smile.

Actually, I feel a lot like smiling. My lips—no, my whole mouth, including my tongue and teeth—are tingling, and my body's on fire. Or melted. I can't tell which. I just know I want to reach for him so badly, to drown my need in him.

"But all that aside. I've been wanting to do that for a long, long time."

Okay, now, *that*'s a surprise. "You *have*?"

"Mmm-hmm. I'm not going to put a date on it, because I don't want to go to jail."

I laugh, and then grind to a halt. "Wait. You're saying you didn't start feeling this way just since I've been back in Rush Creek."

He shakes his head. "Oh, no. Way before that."

Way before? "So why were you always so curt with me?"

He raises his eyebrows like this might be the dumbest question anyone's ever asked. "Self-preservation?"

"I thought you hated me," I admit.

"Oh, Rachel," he says helplessly. "Jesus. No." He closes his eyes and leans his head back against the seat.

"Me too. I mean, I've wanted this for a long time, too."

His eyes pop open. It's his turn to look startled.

"What?" I say. "Did you think I was the one woman who was immune to your charms?"

"I'm not that charming."

Oddly enough, I think he means it.

"You are. And I'm not. Immune. I'm not."

"The point is," he says, "I want to kiss you again."

Ohhh. Okay, then.

"You could," I whisper, unable to look away from his mouth. It's full and soft and I can practically already feel it. The slide of his tongue, the taste of him.

"Don't tempt me."

It's a growl.

"What if..." My breath is a hot mess, rapid and ragged. "What if I want to tempt you?"

"Rachel," he warns. The roughness in his voice does terrible, wonderful things to my nipples, which in turn send a shot of heat to the needy place between my legs. "I think we both know it's a bad idea. You're just off a bad breakup—"

"Connor told you that?"

"Uh-huh. And I'm off a bad breakup."

"I'm sorry. I didn't know." Connor's information stream is one-way, I guess.

He waves a hand, as if to say it doesn't matter, but of course, I'm curious.

"And Connor has been my best friend my whole life."

"Also fair," I say. "But Brody?"

"Yes?" he says.

"I don't care."

And then I kiss him.

Brody

Rachel's mouth is soft and lush and hungry. She kisses me like she can't get enough, moaning her pleasure, and I kiss her right back, licking into the softness, into the wine-taste of her. Her hands come up, thrusting into my hair, and the pull on my scalp tugs a hundred other sensitive places. I was hard before her lips touched mine, but now I'm hard enough that it hurts, the best-ever ache.

She crawls over and straddles me, pressing her heat against my throbbing cock.

Holy shit, she feels good. Her weight where I want it, my hands suddenly filled with her curves. I yank her close, closer, and thrust up against her heat.

She's frantic, tipping her hips, rubbing along my length.

I break the kiss and say, breathless, "Keep that up, and I'm going to come in my pants like a teenager."

"I want that. I want to make you feel good."

"You're already making me feel good. Kiss me again."

We kiss and kiss. I can't get enough. It's a good thing I didn't know any of this about Rachel—how soft her tits feel in my hands; how hard her nipples get when she's turned on, especially in the cool night air; that she whimpers each time she rolls her hips.

I kiss her mouth, slide my lips along her jaw to find her earlobe, soft as satin, and the patch of smooth, tender skin just behind it. I breathe against the shell of her ear, loving the jerk of her hips, her broken moan. With the tip of my tongue, I chase that sensation for her, and am rewarded with more rubbing, more moaning.

She is so fucking hot.

I cup both her breasts in my hands. They overflow my grasp, and it's my turn to moan and jerk against her, involuntarily, and for a second I almost lose control. Then I find it again, and stroke her through her t-shirt, loving the softness, the way her head rolls back and another sound, one I haven't heard before, escapes her lips. A needy little huff of breath.

I'm hungry for more. I yank her shirt up and find her bra underneath, dip my head to lick one hard peak through the thin lace of a bra whose color I can't make out in the dim cab.

"Brody," she pleads, so I lick again, circling, imagining that I can draw the tension there to a perfect, sweet, crisis. With my hand, I work the other nipple, and she finds a steady rhythm against me.

I grasp her hips to make her stop, and she whimpers again. "Please."

"Not yet."

I reach behind her and unhook her bra. The moment I release the strap, she sighs, and when I reach to touch her, both hands on those soft, perfect globes, she makes a strangled sound of pleasure and relief.

I pinch her nipples lightly, so lightly, and work them patiently while I spread my thighs a little to make it impossible for her to rub off on me.

"Stop teasing."

"It's too fun."

"You're killing me."

She reaches between us. For the button of my jeans. Lust makes her clumsy, and she grapples unsuccessfully.

I shake my head.

"I want you," she says. "You've got to have a condom in here somewhere."

I put my hands on her shoulders. Gently. And shift her back, just a little. Using the spread of my thighs and the press of my palms to keep her at a safe distance.

"We should stop."

"I don't want to stop," she says breathlessly, which almost tears through my self-control.

But this is Rachel. *Rachel.*

I've had a lot of sex in trucks, and I'd bet she hasn't had any.

"I don't want to stop either," I say. "I want to know if you'll come like this. My fingers on your nipples and your pussy rubbing off on my cock. I want to know what sounds you make when you come. What you look like. How flushed you get. I want to know if you'll beg me if I take too long."

"I will!" she breathes. "God, Brody. I will!"

"But if I don't stop now, I'm going to end up fucking you in my truck. And you're not that girl."

I'm looking right into her eyes when I say this. It's dark, but even so, I see it.

The flinch.

I feel it, too. She freezes under my hands. Stock still.

Like she went from flame to stone in a second.

I know I've made a big mistake.

"Rachel."

She's shaking her head. She eases off me and turns to

settle herself back in the passenger seat. Even from over here, though, I can feel that sudden stiffness in her body.

"Rachel, talk to me."

For a split, fearful second, I think she won't. And then she crosses her arms, opens her mouth, and unleashes.

I'm really pissed. "That *not that girl* stuff is a load of hooey," I tell him.

My anger is an army revved up for warfare. I can still see Werner's apologetic face and hear him telling me I'm the girl you bring home to your parents. The girl you marry. And all the things I couldn't say to Werner, they're lined up like soldiers, ready to march out for battle.

"I'm not the girl who anything," I say. "I'm Rachel. I'm *this* girl—this *woman*, actually. I like sex, and I think I would probably enjoy getting fucked in a truck, with the right guy."

I note that I just said *fucked* and the world doesn't seem to have ended. Actually, I feel pretty good.

"And FYI, the 'right guy' would *not* be the kind of guy who would tell me I wasn't *that* kind of girl."

Brody winces. "Hey," he says. "I'm sorry. That was a dumbass thing to say."

Oh.

A real apology.

Haven't heard one of those in a long time. Do people even do them anymore?

"Thank you."

We're both quiet for a moment. He's still watching me silently, attentively. Like he heard me. Sees me. As if what I just said makes as much sense in his head as it does in mine. Which may or may not be the case given that I haven't told him yet why those words—"you're not that girl"—made me insta-lose my cool.

"I mean, I get it," I tell him. "You've spent your whole life thinking of me as Connor's little sister."

He opens his mouth to say something, then closes it.

"I'm not. I'm not anyone's little anything."

"No." He shakes his head. "You're not. And Rachel?"

"Yeah?"

"To me, you never have been. And I'm sorry if I made you feel like I thought that."

I'm not sure if it's the apology, his sincerity, or the warmth in his eyes that makes me able to take my first long, deep breath since I started yelling at him, but I do. And then another. The vise around my chest loosens, which is almost worse, because what's left is my hurt feelings.

And the truth.

"I'm not mad at you."

Then I tell him the story.

The whole thing. Not just the version I've told my friends, where I lose my job and then catch my boyfriend cheating, and bummer, as a side effect, no apartment! Not that version, an adult *Alexander and the Terrible, Horrible, No Good, Very Bad Day*. But the whole thing.

I start before work, before the donut. I tell Brody how I woke up that morning and started cleaning the apartment. How I put the roast in the slow cooker. And then Werner came downstairs and offered to make me breakfast, which turned out to be cold cereal with milk. Also, he was already looking at his phone while he was talking to me.

"That *dick*," Brody growls.

I tell him about the part where my boss said I was perfect and let me go anyway, because—I know now—being perfect was never a guarantee of employment or, more to the point, happiness.

The skirt on the floor.

The strength of my denial, how I stared at that skirt and thought up a hundred excuses for it.

I tell Brody about seeing Werner from behind.

Okay, I don't dwell on that, because I don't want him to have nightmares or anything.

I get to the part about the Other Woman. Her ridiculous lace-up teddy and her totally unjustified tears. I don't dwell on that, either, because she doesn't deserve my time or energy.

(Also, it occurs to me as I'm telling the story that I don't own any lingerie other than bras and panties, but I don't mention this.)

Brody doesn't say anything. He just listens and makes sympathetic noises. But his hands?

They're clenched into fists on his thighs.

His perfect, tree-trunk, thighs.

I worry he might break a tooth, the way his jaw is locked tight.

His eyes never leave mine, which is a lot of Brody all at once. I can feel the intensity of his gaze like warm honey trickling down inside me. Licking around my inner thighs and into the melting place between my legs.

It's hard to maintain my outrage at Werner in the face of all that Brody, but I manage.

I tell him that Werner said I was the perfect woman.

"If I'm so perfect," I ask Brody, "why did he pick someone else to stick his dick into?"

Brody makes a sound like he's been punched in the stomach.

"Which means I can't be that perfect, doesn't it? Not *really*."

"Rachel."

I'm shaking my head.

"I'm the girl he wanted to marry. The girl he wanted his parents to meet. But not the girl he wanted to spend a Friday morning messing around with. Not the girl he wanted to have fun with. Not the sexy girl. Not the girl he would choose, if he could choose. Not the girl he'd *be* with, his whole self. Not that girl."

My voice cracks.

Brody reaches out and cups my face, brushing his thumb over my cheek.

I realize he's wiping away a tear.

"That guy," he says steadily. "Is a total fucking *idiot*."

BRODY DRIVES me home after that.

"Hey, Rachel?" he says, when we're parked in my driveway. "Can I ask you a question?"

I nod.

"I had an idea. But I don't know if it'll work."

"Shoot."

"This thing we're doing, the partnership, with you selling on the boat. Do you think we could do it with other things, too? Like, I don't know, the book store? Or people who make jewelry or crafts? They could bring their stuff on board, and you could host, like you do?"

"I think it's brilliant."

Brody's smile starts with his dimple, then the corner of his mouth, then escalates into something even more dangerous than his kisses.

"I've been thinking about going into town, asking some of the businesses to partner with me. Like, maybe tomorrow? Any interest in coming with?"

Brody's super cute when he's like this. Excited and a little shy. Eager to please. Like a kid who isn't used to getting things right.

It's a different side of him from the broody badass, and I totally dig it.

"I'd love that," I tell him, and get another smile.

And another kiss, long and slow and sweet.

It turns dark and needy almost instantly. He cups my head and pulls back. "Rachel," he growls. "Did you do that on purpose? On the boat? Make me think about you with the ben wa balls inside you?"

I smile.

"You are *not* a good girl," he grits out.

"No," I agree, deeply pleased that he knows it.

"I'm going to spend a lot of time thinking about that between today and tomorrow," he says.

Then he kisses me again. Fiercely. And it's so good.

I float up to the house.

14

The next morning—after I sleep too late and bolt down breakfast—Brody pulls into the driveway.

I hurry to the truck and launch myself up into the passenger seat beside him.

Then I die of how good he looks and smells. Like, fresh from the shower, reeking of Irish Spring and Old Spice good. Torn jeans with already-strained denim pulled tight over his quads. And yet another second-skin t-shirt, this one proclaiming, "Real Men Fish."

You'd get more or less the same effect without the text.

He leans over and molds his mouth to mine, and I go from normal woman to melted puddle of need in three seconds flat.

He pulls back and eyes me. I'm breathing hard.

"Ready?" he asks, a flash of green eyes and something that I'm pretty sure is a smirk.

Brody, smirking. This is actually a thing.

This is a very, very good thing.

"Ready," I say.

Or as ready as anyone can ever be for Brody Wilder.

Brody, in typical Brody style, says nothing else to me as we head toward town. After a while, the silence stretches to the breaking point, and as we near the business district, I ask, "So what's the plan?"

"I made a list," he says, rustling along the dash for a piece of paper and dropping it in my lap. "Potential partners."

"What if I want to keep you to myself?"

He barks out a laugh. I've startled him enough that he takes his eyes off the road, and I see them in all their glory. The corner of his mouth stays turned up, too. My thighs jellify.

"From a business perspective," I say, still teasing.

"Mmm-hmm." His eyes are back on the road, but his mouth still quirks like he's holding back a smile. It's delicious. "You won't be here forever."

"True," I say. "So I can't get an exclusive while I'm in town?" And then, when I get another flash of Brody green eyes, "From a business perspective, I mean."

"Not," he says, "from a business perspective. But if you want to talk about a different arena, maybe."

"Brody," I say. "I know I said I don't care about Connor, but—"

He cuts me off. "I'll deal with Connor. He's my problem, not yours."

He pulls into a parking space in front of Krandall's Outdoor Outfitters.

Rush Creek has changed a ton in the time I've lived here. Growing up, it was cowboys and ranchers and outdoor adventurers bound for one of the national forests. These days, it's more of a classic tourist destination, filled with honeymooners and wedding planners, couples on getaway jaunts, and groups of women enjoying girls' weekends away. Stores I took for granted as a kid—like a gift shop that sold rodeo-related trinkets—have been completely transformed. The new tourists wear yoga pants and sports sandals, travel in packs of laughing women, and carry pretty tissue-paper stuffed shopping bags.

It still has more or less the same look—low, saloon-style architecture, Western front porches, barrels and T-shaped light stanchions. Wide plank horizontal wood siding, and here or there something a little more cottage-styled, with flower-boxes in the windows.

I surf a wave of nostalgia as Brody pulls into town. I think basically everyone who grew up in Rush Creek has some longing for the old rodeo, even those of us who thought we were indifferent. It was the heart of the town for so long.

Brody and I hop down from the truck and head into Rush to Read Books. Jem owns the shop; she's my mom's age and they're good friends. She was a second mom to me when I was growing up—or third, if you count Barb Wilder.

Jem comes out from behind the desk to hug me. She's Haitian-American, first generation, with dark cool-brown skin and medium-length straightened hair. She dresses, like my mom, in mom jeans, t-shirts, and sweatshirts—hers with the Rush to Read logo on the front. She and her husband have two teenaged girls who also sometimes work in the shop, although neither of them is here today.

Jem crosses her arms and narrows an eye at Brody. "And this is one of the Wilder boys. Brody, right?"

He's pretty distinctive, even among his brothers. The

tattoos, boots, and cuffs, which have made a return today, are a dead giveaway.

"That's right, ma'am," he says, and shakes her hand. "I'm actually here to make a business proposition."

Her eyes flick to the tattoos and cuffs, but she says, "Go ahead."

"I want to do book clubs on my boat. But it's not my skill set."

Jem, to her credit, just nods at that.

"So I was wondering if you'd want to do it. I could give you a small cut of the trip profits, and everyone would have to buy the book from you."

She sighs. "Brody, my dear, I wish I could help you, but book clubs are tricky with tourists. They're not here long enough to read the book."

I feel a pang of sympathy—shot down so fast on his first attempt—but Brody comes right back at her. "What if you sold them on consignment through the hotel? As people show up, the books are sitting right there, and people can grab a copy. The money still goes to you. They get their copy and sign up to come out on the boat and talk about it. And you host."

Her eyebrows go up. "I thought Gabe was the businessman in your family."

He shrugs. "He is. This is just an idea."

"It's a good one," she says, thoughtfully. "I'm willing to give it a shot."

They talk for a while, working out some of the details, then shake hands. "You should also reach out to the library," she says. "They're always looking for programming ideas. As it gets harder to attract patrons into the library, they're looking for creative ways to reach people. Ask for Donna when you go in there and say Jem sent you."

"Thank you, ma'am," Brody says. "Will do."

Jem turns to me. "How's your mama doing?" she asks. "How's that foot?"

"Healing. Slowly. She's not in nearly as much pain anymore."

"Oh, good," Jem says.

I tell her that while we're in there, I would like to get a couple of books for my mom. "She's going through them like wildfire." I turn to Brody. "If you don't mind?"

He shakes his head. "I'm going to grab a cup of coffee. You want one?"

"Yes, please."

"Jem?"

"Make mine a latte and you're on."

We both try to give him money, but he waves it off and disappears out the front door. I can't help it; I watch him going, admiring the view. Broad back, narrow hips, and a butt that might, with enough exposure, banish my bad Werner memories.

"Those boys," Jem says, shaking her head. "Cutest things on two legs, and the manners! And that one's smart, too. So," she says. "Romance, right?"

My mouth falls open.

"Rachel," she says. "You and your mom want romance books. That was my question. What did you think I was asking?"

But it's pretty obvious, and she doesn't bother to hide her grin.

"When do you have to be back?" I ask Rachel, when we've made the rounds of the shops in town and climbed back into the truck.

"No particular time," she says.

Our rounds in town went really well. People loved the idea of hosting an event on the boat. Kiona of Five Rivers Arts and Crafts said she could do beginning weaving and had friends who might be interested in basketry and simple jewelry-making. Nan from Rush Creek Bakery said she didn't know what services she could provide, but if I was interested in having her prepare baked goods or sandwiches for the outings, she was all in. (I said hell yes.) The day spa signed up for two different events, chair massage and reflexology. They said no to mani pedis because precision's tough on a boat, and I was relieved. And the game store said they had a bunch of simple games that would work even with a breeze.

When people expressed wariness about partnering with me—the game store even brought up my hostile reviews—Rachel stepped in and talked me up. She said I kept the boat clean and well-maintained, was a careful, responsible skipper, and quick on my feet. She told the story of how I'd defused a fight (not getting into the details of how it started), and said I was friendly and easy to work with and that they shouldn't be fooled by how little I talked. That was where *they* came into the deal! she said cheerfully. And there were really positive reviews, too. She pulled out her phone to show them.

Looking at myself, like that, through Rachel's eyes?

I almost didn't recognize myself.

I wondered if that was how people felt after getting makeovers.

"Makeovers on the boat would be really cool," I told Rachel.

"Tricky not to stick an eye pencil in the wrong place," she pointed out. "And the mascara's a nightmare."

"See. This is why I keep you around."

I'm feeling pretty damn pleased with myself, I have to say. My calendar is full of events, basically through the end of tourist season.

And somewhere in the middle of it all, I caught Rachel watching me with this thoughtful expression. Not the look I'm used to seeing on women's faces, which lands right around my center of gravity, with a brief trip up only to make sure there's a face attached to the rest of me.

Rachel's eyes on my face feel like approval in its purest form. As if everything she said out loud, selling my idea, is truth.

Like I said, it's been a long time since anyone looked at me that way.

It feels good, and a little scary.

I don't want it to end.

"We're going for a picnic," I announce. I pull the truck out and point us toward the wilderness.

"Wait!" she says. "We can't just *go* for a picnic. I'm not *ready* for a picnic. I would have dressed differently."

"You're dressed perfectly." My gaze falls to her legs, smooth and warm brown beneath the mid-thigh hem of her sundress. They're slightly paler inside, and my fingertips desperately want to explore that softness.

"And I would have made sandwiches! Or, well, I would have gotten my mom to make Cuban sandwiches." She wrinkles her nose. "And we don't have a blanket. Or water bottles."

I frown. "Rachel, baby. We don't need a plan to have a picnic."

"*I* need a plan to have a picnic."

"Do you trust me?"

There's a long silence. My heart pounds. Then she says, "Yeah. I do."

We pass out of the business district and onto Highway 25. We drive for a while in silence, before she asks, "Where are we going?"

I'm torn between laughing and wanting to reassure her. "I don't know," I tell her, to see how she reacts.

She slumps a little in her seat. "How will we know when we're there?"

Now I do laugh. "I'll know."

"Doesn't that scare you at all?"

I shake my head. Plenty of things scare me, but driving without a map isn't one of them.

We continue in silence, the high desert rolling out on either side of us, brown and sage green.

"Rach?" I ask her.

"Mmm-hmm?"

"Do you always have a plan?"

"Yeah." She's quiet for a sec, then says, "I even had a life plan. Until I got triple whammied."

"Life plan?" I ask. Then, "Triple whammied?" Although I think I know what she means by that.

She makes another hmming noise. "Life plan." She ticks it off on her fingers: "*One*, a four-oh in high school, *two*, college, *three*, grad school, *four*, great apartment, *five*, the library job of my dreams, *six*, awesome boyfriend, *seven*, meet the parents, *eight*, get engaged, *nine*, get married, *ten*, have two-point-five kids, *eleven*, live happily ever after."

"Holy shit, Rachel." Her list hurts my head. And my chest. Though maybe it's not the list that gets to me. Maybe these aches are how I imagine the triple whammy must have felt to her.

"It got blown up, though. My plan. Items four through eleven, obliterated. Triple whammied: job, boyfriend, and apartment in one day."

"I'm sorry," I say. I reach out and put my hand on her thigh. Not to cop a feel, although, God, she's soft. Just to give her comfort.

"Thanks."

I leave my hand there, and she weaves her fingers with mine. It feels so good, I almost drive off the road. I close my hand, squeezing hers.

"It'll be okay," she says, after a moment. "I sent out a bunch of cover letters and resumes yesterday. And Louisa is going to sublet me a room in her apartment."

And you'll find another awesome boyfriend.

I hate the idea, even though I'm pretty sure I wouldn't qualify as *awesome boyfriend* according to the Master Plan's criteria. I almost ask what they are, then decide I don't need to rain on our picnic. She's here with me today, we're both in good moods, and I'm going to show her some of my favorite things. Then I'll make her cry my name in the open air. That's all the plan I need.

"I've never had a plan," I tell her.

"For anything?"

"I mean, sometimes I have a plan for a day. But not usually."

Of course, not having a plan doesn't mean you can't get triple whammied.

I don't say that out loud.

We've been driving thirty or so minutes when I spot what we need. It's a roadside stand, the semi-permanent variety. I haven't seen this particular one before, but I would have been willing to swear we'd come across something like it. We pull into the gravel-and-overgrown-grass parking lot.

"Elk jerky," Rachel reads off the hand-spray-painted sign. "Buffalo jerky. Beef jerky."

"Mmm-hmm," I say. "And cherries. For lunch."

"That's not lunch," she says, but she's definitely smiling.

"Do you not like elk jerky?"

"I do like it, actually."

"Cherries?"

"Love 'em."

I buy a bunch of both and a couple of bottles of water. "Lunch," I say, holding the paper bag out to Rachel. "Do you have any paper towels?" I ask the cowboy behind the stand.

He tears a bunch off a roll and hands them over.

I take the opportunity to inspect the back of the truck. There's no blanket, but there's a scruffy blue tarp that hasn't seen too much wear and tear. "Will this do?" I ask Rachel.

"Yeah." She's definitely smiling.

I pull her close and kiss her nose. She lifts her chin and our mouths meet, a soft settling into each other.

I could kiss her for hours, but I let her go as another car pulls into the parking lot.

"Anything else worrying you?" I ask her.

She shakes her head.

"See?" I say. "No plan, no problem."

Brody turns down a side road that gives way to dirt.

"Were you messing with me when you said you didn't know where you were going and would know when we got there?" I ask.

"'Fraid so," he says.

I punch his arm, and he laughs. It's a pure, rich, molasses sound, and I want to wrap myself up in it.

He drives down the road until he reaches a gate, then parks. We're the only vehicle here. I think we're in the low foothills of the Cascades, but geography has never been my strong suit, and I was too busy freaking out to keep track of how we got here.

He pulls the tarp from the truck bed.

"Can you walk a couple hundred yards?"

I glance down at my sandaled feet. These are relatively sturdy sandals, the kind you could walk around town in, or Disneyland for a day, but I'm not sure how well they'll do with the woods.

"It's just like this," he says, gesturing at the ground, which is a cat track. "No rougher."

That turns out to be true; I get a few pebbles in my sandals, and my toes are dusty, but that's the worst of it. And it's worth it when we step out into an open area, a high rock outcropping overlooking a lake. The lake is a beautiful ice-blue color, surrounded by sunlit trees.

"Oh!" My voice reveals my delight. "This is beautiful!"

He spreads the tarp out. I look down at my dress, and at the tarp, which is—to put it kindly—dusty. Then I sit, because, well, *dang it all to heck*, as they say. My dress will launder, and Brody is right. I never do anything without a plan, and it feels good.

Besides, the dirt on the tarp is nothing compared to what the cherry juice is going to do to my white, yellow, and orange sundress. We sit side by side, facing the water. When Brody puts an arm around me, I scooch closer to him. He's warm and muscly. My body gears up for more of that goodness by melting.

We eat jerky and cherries and drink water. The salty-sweet combo is so good, I can't stop.

"This is really great, Brody," I say, after a while. "Like, really great."

I get a Brody smile.

"I know," he says. "Do you think it would have been better if we planned it?"

I punch him. Mostly because his arm is like a brick wall, and it's satisfying. Then I relent and say, "Nope."

He kisses me with his salty-sweet mouth. Then he draws back and strips off his shirt.

"That's pretty forward, don't you think?" I tease.

He tosses his shirt on the tarp, and I stop teasing because, wow.

The last time I saw Brody without his shirt was years ago. He was, maybe, sixteen. And it was a beautiful sight then. But now? He's a wall of tanned, muscled perfection. Broad shoulders, cut, inked pecs, ridged abs, just the right amount of dark-gold chest hair, and a matching trail disappearing into his jeans.

"See something you like?" he asks, amused.

I put a hand out and stroke the pretty. His abs flex under my touch, a small groan escaping his mouth. He captures my hand with his as I find his waistband.

"I want to show you one of my favorite things," he says, stripping off his jeans. Now I really can't take my eyes off him. He's wearing gray cotton boxer briefs, and my touch has apparently positively affected him, because—yeah. The bad boy is big.

"I want to see it."

His eyes follow my gaze and darken, but he says, "You can see that later."

"I'm going to hold you to that."

"Ah, Rachel," he says. "If I'd had any idea how much fun you'd turn out to be, we would have been doing this years ago. C'mere." He leads me to the edge of the rock outcropping we're sitting on.

"We're going to jump."

"Are you out of your mind?" I demand, stepping back from the vertiginous drop.

"Nope," he says. "Do you want to go first, or should I?" His eyes rake over me, appreciative. "You could lose the dress."

"What if someone comes out here?"

"I bet your underwear's pretty."

I roll my eyes at him. "There is no earthly way I'm jumping off that cliff."

"Okay," he says, and shrugs. "See you in a few!"

And with that, he's gone over the edge, yelling.

"Brody!" I call. My stomach lurches, and I peek over the edge, my heart pounding. But when I look down, he's in the water, pumping his fist and howling with joy. It's as much emotion as I've ever seen Brody express, and it fills me with delight.

"It's so awesome!" he yells up to me. "Join me!"

It's like there are two parts of me, the one whose heart took flight over the edge when Brody jumped, full to the brim with Brody's happiness.

And the other part, which is full of objections: things that could go wrong, reasons I need more time to think about this. Like, a year.

Maybe if I'd known ahead of time. If I'd worn a bathing suit. If I had a towel.

If I knew the temperature of the water...

"You don't need a plan! Just do it!" Brody calls.

I feel *seen*.

I'm not sure I can totally explain what happens next.

Or, well, maybe I can.

Most likely, the part of me that's full of Brody pushed the other part of me off the cliff.

I slide the straps of my sundress off my shoulder. I let the dress pool at my feet, exposing my underwear. It's nothing special, but it's not granny panties either. A nice pair of light brown cotton bikinis and a matching lace bra.

Good.

I take a tentative step toward the edge, close my eyes, and jump.

17

BRODY

S he does it. I hardly have time to think, *She's naked!* And *No, she's wearing a bra and panties!* before she's in the water, hooting and hollering.

"I did it!" she says, breathless. "Oh my God, Brody, I did it!"

I swim over to her. It's not easy to kiss while treading water, but we manage a short, breathless, tantalizing taste.

"See that rock there? That's where we're going. And then there's a path back up."

We swim to the rock, and I boost her up, shamelessly loving the feel of her cool, smooth skin under my rough palms. I climb up on the rock beside her, and she sits close to me, tucking herself into me.

"Rachel," I whisper.

She turns towards me and tips her face up, so trusting and eager that my cock manages to rally against the icy dip, reaching for her.

This woman.

I kiss her. She tastes so good, sweet and salty and *Rachel,* which is definitely the best of those three flavors. And she is soft in my arms—hair damp against my cheek, satiny arms wrapped around my neck, breasts pillowed against my chest.

I kiss along her jaw, tease her ear, kiss down her throat, to the hollow. I lick that spot until her cries turn to pleas. I drop kisses along her collarbone.

Then I lean back, slightly, and take a minute to just soak her in.

"Fucking A, Rachel. You're so beautiful." I stare, shamelessly, because *holy shit* she's gorgeous. Smooth-as-satin skin, spilling out of the lacy cups of her bra, curving down over her belly to the triangle of her bikini, through which I can see the tantalizing shadow of her pussy. I duck my head and kiss her everywhere, open mouthed, tongue exploring her. I tease the edge of lace with the curled tip of my tongue and she makes a perfect, helpless noise that I feel like it's the tug of a hand on my cock. No, that *is* her palm on my cock, cupping me, pressing me. I reach down, nudge her hand aside, because this is for her.

Then I go back to work, running my lips and tongue over every exposed bit of her. Edging the cup of her bra down, I find her nipple with a biting tease. I flick it with the tip of my tongue, over and over, until she pants and clutches my head. Sliding off the rock, I help her wiggle to the edge, then kneel between her legs and slide my hands up her thighs.

My mouth follows my hands, tasting the smooth bare skin, finding her panties with my thumbs. I dip my head and suck, then open my mouth over her to breathe heat against her mound.

"Brody!"

"You want more?"

"Yes!"

"Lean back. Open your legs."

I watch her face, registering the flare of her pupils. She likes the command. Noted.

Then she sits straight up, and for a split, wretched second, I think she's calling it.

But nope. She slides her panties down. She slips them off, folds them, and sets them on the rock next to her.

Those two things—her baring herself to me, and the care she takes with it—make my chest hurt.

Then all the ache shifts to another part of me, because I'm looking at her, and she's so fucking pretty. A neatly trimmed strip of dark curls, her clit swollen enough to peek out at me, and her lips glistening and eager.

I need to get my mouth on her.

She tastes so good. She's so soft and so lickable and I want all of her. I need to get my tongue on her clit, need to give it the same pleasure I gave her nipple, nipping and flicking and drawing all those little gasps and pleas from her lips. I have to see how she likes it. Whether she wants the tip or the flat, the flicks or the circles, fast, slow, up and down. Just right here, or the feel of my whole mouth, open and hungry, over all of her.

News flash: She likes it all.

She lifts her hips and jerks against me, grabs my hair and calls my name.

"You need more?"

"Yes, please."

The *please* slays me. *Jesus, Rachel.*

She's tight. Slick and tight. My cock clenches at the root and there's a split second when I think I'm going to lose it. Then I get myself under control. I work my finger gently into her, and she squeezes it, thrusting back against my hand. I lick her harder, faster, and she replies, *yes, please*, this time with the rocking of her hips.

"More?"

"Brody," she gasps, which I take as a another yes.

I love all her yesses.

I give her a second finger. An open-mouthed kiss and a long, flat lick. And with a cry, she tips over the edge, coming, clenching my fingers, writhing against my tongue, calling my name.

I lift my head, letting my hand do the work my tongue was doing, because I need to see her face.

And I'm so glad I do, because she's even prettier like this, all undone, head thrown back, mouth open, eyes closed, cheeks flushed.

I start to move away, to stand up and help her put herself back together.

"No. Wait."

She reaches for me.

"Rachel—"

"Please. Just let me."

No argument here. She runs a thumb over my boxer-briefs, over the swollen head of my cock, then untangles me from my shorts.

"You have a nice cock," she says, which catches me somewhere right between a chuckle and a shudder of pleasure. And then she wraps her hand around it, cool and sure, and her fingers are way prettier there than on that silicone model I've seen her handle. It probably would have been enough to put me within three strokes of bliss, even before she pulls her hand back, licks her palm, and goes to work again.

The sexiest part is that she's watching, too, watching her hand fist my cock, my head emerge, shiny and taut, a new droplet forming. Her lips are parted, her tongue peeking out.

"Rachel." My voice breaks.

She opens her eyes.

"You might want to—"

I'm not sure what I was going to say. *Stop*, maybe, or *duck*, or *grab a paper towel.*

But Rachel has the situation in hand—literally. "Shhh," she says. "I gotcha."

Some guarded thing in me lets go, and suddenly I'm coming in long shuddering waves, lashing her palm. It's one of those deep orgasms, the ones that feel ripped up from the bottom of your spine, that go on and on in waves.

My knees buckle and I lower myself to the rock beside her, pulling her closer.

She tilts her face up and smiles at me, shy and real. "Never a dull moment."

Then she leans her head on my shoulder, her hands still cupping me, and makes a small humming sound, like happiness.

Me fucking too, Rachel, I think. *Me fucking too.*

18

We clean up, then dry off in the sun, then get dressed and pack up our picnic. I'm relaxed and contented, and haven't thought for hours about the train wreck that is my old life.

We must have been out of cell phone range for a while, because as we get close to Rush Creek and home, all of a sudden, my phone chirps and coughs up a whole bunch of notifications. Texts, from Louisa, from my mom, from Amanda. I sift through them—nothing essential. Louisa wants to know what's up with the bad boy, my mom tells me one of my cousins is passing through tonight on a trip from the Redwood National Forest to Seattle and she's making ropa vieja so I should be back by 7:30 and hungry, and Amanda is nailing down our plans for tomorrow night. *Can you meet at Oscar's at 7?* she wants to know.

Then I get distracted by a voicemail. From Hettie at the library.

"I'm just going to listen to this voicemail. It's from my ex-boss."

"Sure." Brody hums, tapping his fingers on the steering wheel. Not scowling, not at all. I smile, too, thinking of how totally bowled over he looked after I made him come. Gratitude is hot.

Rachel, the voicemail says. *Don't hang up on me, even though I know you might be tempted. We can give you your job back.*

I think I make a small, startled sound, because Brody's eyes leave the road and find my face for a second, making sure everything's okay. I smile, signaling that it is, but he still looks concerned, and his hand finds my thigh again.

I like them both, that concern and that hand on my thigh.

I listen to the rest of Hettie's explanation, which is long and complicated and concludes with, *Call me first thing Monday.*

Right, the call came in on East Coast time right around five p.m. on a Friday. Not gonna learn anything more till Monday.

"They can give me my job back," I tell Brody.

His eyes leave the road again. "What?"

"So apparently one of my coworkers gave notice yesterday and they can reallocate her position as long as I'm willing to leave children's for adult, which I totally am. So I have my job back!"

"That's great!" Brody says. "You must be psyched."

"Uh—" I say.

To be honest, I can't figure out what I'm feeling. Relieved? Maybe. I mean, this is huge, right? Basically, the plan is back on track, minus Werner, and the only way to think about Werner is as a wrong turn.

But I am enjoying my strange Rush Creek detour. This

time out of time, nothing happening the way I expect. There's something about knowing it will end—and how—that is disappointing.

"I think I'm not quite ready for my vacation to be over," I tell Brody. That's a thing, right? Of course it is. And as soon as I say it, I feel better, because no one *wants* to go back to work.

I hadn't realized Brody was tensed up, but when I say that, his jaw loosens a bit and his shoulders drop.

"I'm not ready for it to be over either," he says, and his fingers tighten on my thigh. I can feel the echo of that all the way in my core, and my clit perks up.

"Either way, I have to stay till my mom's foot is healed," I remind him.

But it's only two more weeks until the date the doctor threw out to her, and suddenly that doesn't feel like very long.

I squeeze Brody's hand, and he flips his hand to squeeze mine back.

I remember that I never responded to Amanda.

"I have to text your sister. We're having dinner tomorrow night."

Brody's eyes meet mine again, startled. "Wait, what?" He pulls into my parents' neighborhood as I text Amanda back, *Yes, perfect, can't wait.*

"Amanda and Lucy and Hanna and I are having dinner tomorrow night." I glance at him to find him staring at me with a look I can only describe as horror. "What? Is that bad?"

"No," he says, and then, more firmly, "no. It's good. They're good people. Have a good time. Say hi from me. If Easton's there, don't talk to him."

"What?"

"He'll flirt with any woman with a pulse, and he's especially prone to trying to seduce women his brothers are interested in. We've almost disowned him several times, but he's such a magnet, we can't afford not to keep him around."

I giggle.

He pulls into my driveway and parks, then leans over and kisses me. Hard. Sweeping his tongue into my mouth, cupping my head, leaving me breathless.

Drawing back, he smiles at me. "Damn. Now I don't want you to get out of the truck."

"My cousin's coming for dinner and my mom made ropa vieja, so I have to. But I'll see you Sunday. For a Perez-Wilder family dinner."

"Oh, right," he says. "Oh. That'll be—challenging. Maybe I should just tell Connor before that so we don't have to pretend nothing's going on."

I tilt my head. "Is it worth telling him, when I'm leaving?"

Brody scowls, which he hasn't done for a while. And I have to admit, as much as I love his smile, I love his scowl, too. "I guess not," he says. "Why rock the boat when it doesn't have to be rocked?"

I give him one more kiss, then exit the truck. As I'm walking around it to the house, he lowers the window and calls, "Rach."

"Yeah?"

"When you go out with the girls tomorrow night?"

"Mmm-hmm?"

"Don't believe everything they tell you."

Then he drives away.

I replay that line in my head a bunch of times.

He doesn't sound like he's teasing.

19

RACHEL

I push open the door at Oscar's Saloon & Grill, searching for Amanda, Hanna, and Lucy.

Oscar's was my favorite restaurant as a kid. I used to beg to go there. I always ordered the same thing: a bacon cheeseburger with extra fries.

It hasn't changed much. It still has the swinging saloon doors, the big mural of cowboys on the dusty main street of old Rush Creek, the moose and elk heads mounted over the bar.

They've refreshed some of the decor, but those parts have stayed the same, and I get a warm, homey feeling when I step in, which is intensified when Hanna, Lucy, and Amanda all wave me over to their table.

I'm a little nervous about going out for drinks with Amanda because of the whole bagged-her-brother dynamic. What gives me courage is the fact that Lucy is Gabe's girlfriend, and that doesn't seem to have kept her and Amanda from becoming chummy.

I'm also on edge because of the cryptic thing Brody said

last night when he dropped me off, about not believing everything they said. What was that about?

Amanda and Lucy greet me warmly, and I return their hugs and hellos. Hanna, who hasn't left her seat, grunts hello, then says, "Has someone briefed her on the rules?"

Amanda and Lucy roll their eyes. "Hanna is here provisionally," Amanda says. "She'll leave if we talk about anything girly." She frowns. "Han, does that include vibrators? Because I can't promise not to ask Rachel important questions about vibrators."

She says this last part like the words start with capital letters: Important Questions About Vibrators.

"Hell no," Hanna says. "There's nothing girly about vibrators. They're God's gift to clitorises."

Lucy's eyes meet mine, and I see the question in them —*Are you okay with this madness?*

I smile and shrug, and she grins back at me.

Amanda sets her drink on the table. "Good, because honestly, Hanna, if you shut down the vibrator talk, I was going to make you leave."

Hanna gives Amanda the finger and Amanda smiles sweetly back.

"Happy to answer any and all questions," I say.

"Excellent!" Amanda beams.

Just then, our waitress comes to the table, a pretty young woman with dark hair and big blue eyes. She is super familiar—I think she might have been in the class ahead of me at school. Her nametag says "Jill."

"Jill, this is—"

"You're Connor's sister, right?"

I nod. "Rachel."

"Jill Cooper," she says. "I was a year ahead of your brother in school. But I knew who he was."

"Sadly, I think everyone in your class knows who Connor is." I give her a what-can-you-do look.

As juniors, Connor and Brody crashed the senior prom, got caught drinking, and were suspended from school. (To their credit, they did not and were not planning to drive.) Later, they were also both suspended for stealing the giant stallion statue from the entrance to the football field and putting it in the principal's office.

Then there was the incident where Connor and his friends laid down bubble wrap on all the high school floors, but by that time, Brody had dropped out.

It's actually kind of a miracle Connor graduated, but he managed it.

She smiles. "He and Brody kept things interesting."

Amanda asks Jill about her boyfriend, a guy named Matt who is on the verge of proposing to her but hasn't yet. Jill is getting impatient with him.

"Send yourself flowers from another guy," Amanda advises.

"Does that shit actually work?" Hanna scrunches up her forehead so her eyebrows disappear under her short bangs. That pixie cut is so adorable on her, although I imagine she'd kick my butt if I said so out loud.

"I don't know if it works." Amanda tilts her head. "I've never tried it. Maybe I should."

Jill laughs. "I think I just need to be patient. Knowing Matt, he's waiting for the right moment. One of my rings went missing for a couple of weeks, so that's a good sign, right?"

"Definitely," Amanda says.

Jill takes my drink order and asks us what appetizers we want. When she tucks her notebook away, Amanda tells her our fingers are crossed for her and that we want to know as soon as he pops the question.

"Okay," says Amanda, when she's gone. "Thing one is, when are you going to do a party for us?"

"Whenever you want me to," I say. "Pick a date and we'll do it."

"Thing number two is, how on earth did you convince Brody to still do the party on his boat once he realized what Real Romance sells?"

I've been waiting to give her crap about this. "I can't believe you *knew* he didn't know, and you didn't tell him."

It's Amanda's turn to get wide-eyed. "Gabe was going to tell him," she says slowly.

I stare at her. She stares back.

"He didn't, did he," she says. It's not a question.

I shake my head.

We both look at Lucy, who is legitimately irate. "He told me he told Brody!"

Amanda's mouth is open. "Brothers." Her voice is thick with disgust.

"Are you surprised?" Hanna crosses her arms. "A Wilder brother had a chance to mess with another Wilder brother, and he *took it*. It would be much more surprising if Gabe *had* told Brody and ruined all the fun."

Amanda rolls her eyes. "So you're telling me that Brody showed up, not knowing you were going to whip out dildos?"

"That's what I'm telling you," I say.

"Back up a second," Amanda says. "I need an in-depth, frame by frame, moment by moment, blow by blow—no pun intended—re-creation of the moment Brody realized you were selling eight-inch silicone cocks on his boat."

"I mean, they're not all eight inches," I point out, trying not to think about eight inches I have recently become acquainted with. Must. Not. Think. About. Brody's. Cock.

It's like telling yourself not to think about elephants.

"Okay. Five-inch pink latex dildos, I don't care, please, please, just tell me exactly what the expression on his face looked like."

I flash back to the expression Brody wore when Jack Buddy was on display. And discover I'm blushing. Fiercely. Dagnabbit.

Amanda's eyebrows go up. So do Lucy's.

"I mean, he was definitely surprised," I say, as quickly as I can, but I'm not fooling anyone, except maybe Hanna.

Then I glance at Hanna and discover that she's looking back at me with her mouth open.

So, yeah, not fooling anyone.

"Wait." Amanda puts up a finger. "Wait a second. You... and... Brody?"

My face gets even hotter. "You don't really want to talk about this, do you?" I ask Amanda. "He's your *brother*."

"Oh, yes, she does," Hanna says. "There is no one more interested in the Wilder brothers' romantic adventures than Amanda-formerly-Wilder. She's in the business of procuring cousins for her kids as fast as she possibly can."

"No pressure," Lucy says, making a wry face at me.

"I mean, this is just—I'm only—it's a—"

Yeah, that sentence isn't coming out so well, and they all look faintly amused, probably because at this point my face is the same color as Lucy's Bloody Mary.

"If you're about to say you're only in town for a few weeks, don't bother," Hanna says, tipping her head in Lucy's direction.

I try again, because despite the sheer goodness of things with Brody—and when I say *things*, I mean naughty naked *things*—and despite Brody's best efforts to un-plan me, I do need to go back to my life in Boston. Now that I have my job back, it's kind of a fait accompli.

"I really am *not* staying," I say. "Anyway, Brody doesn't strike me as the marrying kind."

"You'd think, right?" Amanda says.

"He was going to marry Zoë." Hanna hefts her beer stein and swigs.

Amanda's eyes suddenly shoot daggers.

Wait. *What*? "Zoë?"

"Justin's mom," Hanna explains.

Amanda's stare gets even darker, but Hanna is obviously not easily intimidated. "Justin is Brody's kid," she elaborates.

"Wait, Brody has a kid?" I ask.

Brody, like my Brody? The bad boy with the tattoos on the motorcycle? Has. A. Kid?

Don't believe everything they tell you, I can hear him saying. Guess he knew this was going to come out tonight.

Why didn't he tell me himself? I hunch my shoulders against the hurt.

Amanda sighs. "Yeah. Six months old. Cutest thing you've ever seen."

"Connor's never mentioned—"

"It's complicated," Amanda says. She doesn't sound angry, but there's something in her tone that's final.

Conversation over.

What's not over is the unsettled feeling it leaves me with.

Lucy jumps in, addressing Amanda, which I think is her way of changing the subject. "So how are things going with expanding your catering business to dinner orders?"

Amanda starts talking animatedly about how well the catering is going, and my mind wanders to the "bar brawl" I saw Brody get into last month when I was home for my mom's birthday. At the time, I'd felt sad for him. *Brody Wilder, still up to his old antics.* Part of me was disappointed, the part that had wanted to believe he'd left behind his high school self—the guy who pulled pranks for the thrill of them, picked fights, and let himself get drawn into scuffles.

My parents used to say Brody was fighting a war no one could see.

I wonder if his bar brawl was part of that fight.

I wonder if Connor knows what happened between Brody and his ex—if Brody talks to Connor about it.

Jill brings drinks and appetizers. I haven't had cracklings —fried pork rinds—for a few years ago now, and I chow down happily.

"Hey, I hope this is okay to say." Lucy touches my hand again. "But Amanda hinted that you'd been through some tough stuff lately and that you might want to hear my story."

Hanna scoffs. "Amanda doesn't *hint*."

"I was very hint-y in this case," Amanda protests. "I just told Luce that Rachel might appreciate knowing what brought Lucy to Rush Creek."

"I would love to hear what brought you to Rush Creek," I tell Lucy.

She grins at me. Under other circumstances, she's the kind of woman I might find intimidating. She looks—expensive. Her clothes are fashionable and perfectly assembled. She's wearing heels even though we're surrounded by people for whom a fleece jacket and jeans is the new business suit. And she has that kind of glossy hair that forms perfect ringlets when you curl it, which she obviously has for our otherwise casual girls' night.

Also, she's wearing makeup. The only other makeup at the table is Amanda's—a little bit of mascara and lip gloss.

I can do all that stuff—nice clothes, makeup, hair—but in reality? I almost never do. I'm so out of practice, I'm not sure I'd know where to start.

It might be nice to have a friend who could show me if I needed help....

Then I remember I'm not staying in Rush Creek, so Lucy can't be that friend.

Lucy tells me her story—about how a one-night stand blew up her work life and the subsequent implosion dropped her in Rush Creek. She ended up working on a plan to save Wilder Adventures—the plan that, among other things, led to Brody hosting girls' nights.

Gabe apparently wasn't a big fan of Lucy's plan at first—and I sense there's a whole story behind that, but just as I'm about to ask, Lucy shifts her attention to me. "What about you?"

I'm hit with a painful flashback to That Day.

"Unless you don't want to talk about it," she says gently.

"No," I say. "It's helpful to talk about it." I sigh. "In my case, it was my work life that blew up my sex life."

I tell them the story—Amanda's already heard it, but Hanna and Lucy haven't—of how I came home early because

I'd been fired and walked in on Werner and The Woman, which is how I think of her.

"The Woman, by the way, turns out to be someone Werner met when he was out for drinks with co-workers." And then I supply a piece of intel I intercepted earlier this afternoon: "Facebook says they're dating."

They all curse out Werner colorfully, and I appreciate it.

"You're lucky you saw his ass now," Amanda says.

I wince at the image that pops into my head, but she's so right.

They ask what I'm doing about my job, and I tell them about the call I got from Hettie.

"So you're definitely going back," Amanda says.

"I mean, yeah. Rush Creek was never for me."

As soon as the words come out of my mouth, I feel like I need to clarify them, since I'm surrounded by women who've made Rush Creek their home, but as I open my mouth, Amanda waves me off.

"Don't," she says. "We get it. It's not for everyone, small town life."

"I didn't think it was for me," Lucy said. "I thought I was a New York girl through and through."

"How has it been?" I ask before I can stop myself.

Lucy smiles a sweet, secret smile. "Turns out I'm a small town girl after all."

Amanda eyes her drink and her clothes. "You're like a hybrid model. New York tastes, small town heart."

Lucy laughs at that.

Jill shows up again, wanting to know if we want to order entrees or are ready to skip straight to dessert. That's an easy question for all of us—Oscar's has the best chocolate cake in the known universe—and Jill leaves to grab us four slices. She's back moments later, and we all dig in with gusto.

So. Good.

"Cakegasm!" says Amanda. "And speaking of such things. Vibrators. Tell me everything I need to know."

I've just stepped out of the shower late Saturday afternoon, ready to roll to family dinner and a night of pretending not to want to lick Rachel all over, when my phone rings.

It's Zoë.

Instantly my heart starts pounding, because Zoë never calls anymore. All I can think is that something bad has happened to Justin.

Then I remember that Justin isn't my responsibility.

A sour pool forms in the pit of my stomach—but it doesn't make my heart slow down. Now I'm scared shitless for Justin *and* sad.

I guess it's not so easy to stop loving a kid, just because he isn't yours.

"'Lo?" I answer the phone.

"Brody?"

Zoë's voice is low and unalarmed, and I take my first breath since the phone buzzed. "Yeah?"

"I need a favor."

"What's that?"

"I need you to take Justin tonight."

I waited for a text last night from Rachel, letting me know that Amanda or Hanna or Lucy had spilled the beans about Zoë and Justin, but it never came.

I don't know whether that's because they didn't tell her or because she didn't want to ask me about it, but the idea of showing up at Gabe's with Justin feels totally overwhelming.

I already have to pretend about Rachel.

Pretending about Justin *to* Rachel feels like more than I can handle.

"Justin isn't my job anymore, Zoë."

"I know, Brody. I'll pay you. To babysit."

That sits even worse with me. To be paid to babysit for the kid I held in my arms when he was newborn and red-faced? The kid I watched while he slept, my breath syncing with his, and rocked for hours when he couldn't sleep? "No fucking way."

"Just this once, Brody, please. My girlfriends are going to the casino, and I haven't been out in so long. I'm dying."

"Ask your mom."

"She and my dad are in California."

"Where the fuck is Len?"

"He's..." She hesitates. "He went back to his wife."

I close my eyes.

I want to hit someone. Preferably Len Dix. Of course, I've already done that once.

Rachel was there that night. She saw me lose my shit. That's the only thing I regret about hitting Len. I'd do it again in a heartbeat. The feel of my knuckles connecting with his nose was beyond satisfying.

I rub a thumb over my knuckles.

I relished that bruise for days, but I wish Rachel hadn't seen me out of my head with drink and grief and rage.

In the background, I hear Justin. Babbling. He sounds like he's giving a speech, holding forth on something. And suddenly I want to see him. To hold him up over my head, nuzzle his belly, make him laugh that fat, jolly baby laugh of his.

I want it more than I care about my pride.

"Okay," I say.

"Please, Brody," she says, at the same time, because she obviously wasn't expecting me to say yes.

"I said okay. Are you two alone there right now? I'll come get him."

"Yeah. I'll pack up an overnight bag for him. And the port-a-crib."

"I don't need the crib."

"He needs a crib," she says.

"I have a crib."

It comes out like a confession. It is. I'll admit it: I bought a crib for Justin to sleep in even though I'm not his dad, even though I'll never be his dad.

I guess I knew that someday soon Zoë would ask this favor of me, and there was no fucking way I'd be able to refuse.

SHE COMES to the door with Justin and his face lights up when he sees me, which fucking kills me. It's been at least a few weeks since I laid eyes on him, and he still looks utterly delighted. He holds out his arms and I take him from Zoë. He reaches up and takes a handful of my nose, then face plants in my cheek.

"He's started doing that. My mom says he's giving kisses."

My chest hurts so bad. I touch Justin's cheek. It's made of satin, the softest fucking thing I've ever touched. Also a little sticky. Zoë is a good mom, but wiping Justin's face isn't one of her strengths. "Can you bring me a warm, wet washcloth?" I ask her.

To my surprise, she does it without getting defensive. We argued a lot when Justin was a newborn, which maybe should have been my first sign that we weren't all headed for domestic bliss. But we felt like a family and I wanted us to be a family so badly that I was willing to ignore all the warning signs.

I wonder if we would have lasted, if Justin had really been mine. We'd only been together a couple of months when he was conceived. We barely knew each other.

I just didn't realize exactly how little we knew each other.

I clean Justin's chubby face, while he twists and whines in protest, then hand the washcloth back to Zoë.

She looks as tired as she did in Oscar's the other night. She's pretty—dark hair, pale skin, and a body that's snapped back well from pregnancy with Justin—but when I look at her now, I can't remember what drew me to her. It's like someone hollowed out that part of my brain.

"Is the car seat installed?" she asks.

"Yeah. I did it before I drove over here."

I was surprised to discover I still remembered exactly how to do it. Then again, I'd installed car seats in both Zoë's car and mine, and then in her mom and dad's cars, my mom's car, and Amanda's car.

My mom and Amanda have been asking constantly to see Justin.

Well, now they will.

It's a relief of sorts, because it postpones my having to explain why I can't bring Justin around anymore.

I need to explain, though.

I just can't imagine saying the words.

She cheated on me, and it turns out Justin is Len's.

I remind myself that if I don't tell them myself, they're going to find out some other way. My siblings are too connected to the rumor factory of this town for it to stay a secret for long, now that people are talking.

Justin hangs on my hair and bounces up and down, babbling. Drool runs down his face.

"Is he teething?"

She nods. "I put the baby Tylenol in the diaper bag." She bends down, picks up the diaper bag, and puts it over my shoulder for me.

It feels all wrong, now. I don't want her touching me.

"Thank you," she says.

I can tell she means it.

"Yeah."

I turn and go out.

I don't say *you're welcome.*

Once again, Amanda and I stand on Gabe's porch, hashing out dates for a get-together, this time the Real Romance party I'm doing for her, Hanna, Lucy, and their friends.

My dad is inside, cooking with a whole bevy of wickedly attractive Wilders. We usually do lechon asado when we're with them, but we've had a lot of Cuban food lately so we decided to do homemade pizza. The amount of dough rising in Gabe's kitchen is truly epic.

Connor and Amanda's husband Heath are having some kind of hard core conversation about the latest Star Wars movie. I don't pretend to understand, but they've always nerded out on sci-fi stuff and sometimes they get together and play video games.

My mom is sitting on the back deck with her foot up, as she should be.

The one conspicuous absence is Brody, and I haven't wanted to ask anyone where he is. Even Connor. Especially Connor.

We settle on a date, and Amanda tucks her phone into her back pocket just as a truck pulls into the driveway—Brody's. He hops down, then opens the backseat and leans in.

He emerges with his arms full of—

Baby.

That must be baby Justin.

Justin is peak baby right now—fat cheeks, drool, and babble. And the man holding him is peak man: broad shouldered, forearms flexing from the effort of containing his squirming cargo, and stubble-jawed.

Even as confused and hurt as I am, my ovaries go up in smoke.

I discover I'm walking toward the dynamic duo. I hazard a quick glance back at Amanda and she raises an eyebrow at me and smirks.

I can't even care.

God, he looks good. Now that I know how that mouth feels on my body and my hands feel wrapped around his—

Apparently, you can't put that genie back in the bottle.

Which I guess means I'll have to ask it for more wishes.

"Hey," I say.

"Hey."

"You have, um, some secrets."

He nods. His eyes scrape my face. I think he's trying to suss how how mad I am. "I didn't mean to not tell you. It's just really fucking complicated. Oh. God. Sorry dude," he says to Justin, and I can't help it, I laugh.

"You maybe want to tell me the story later?"

"Yeah," he says. "I actually really fucking do. Damn it. Fuck. Sorry, Justin."

"You, um, might want to work on that," I say, smiling.

He smiles, too. "You could help me."

I nod. "I mean, if we hang out long enough, either you're going to become a Puritan or I'm going to start swearing up a blue streak."

"So true."

Neither of us says that two weeks probably isn't long enough for that conversion to take place.

We stand there awkwardly for a moment, until Justin leans forward in his dad's arms, gives me a gummy, one-toothed smile and reaches out a hand.

"Hey, little man," I say to him.

"This is Justin," Brody says, and pride shines all over his face.

"He's adorable. Will he come to me? Is that okay?" I hold out my arms, and Brody transfers Justin into my arms.

I sneak another peek back at Amanda, but she has disappeared. It's just Brody, Justin, and me out here.

Justin is grabbing for everything his chubby little hands can reach—my hair, my earrings, my nose—and talking up a blue streak in nonsense syllables.

"Do you have him for the weekend?" I make goofy open-mouthed faces at Justin, and he chortles. Baby chortles! They're the best.

"Just tonight. You look beautiful."

I look up from Justin's beaming face and into Brody's. He's not scowling, but he's Brody-serious. Intense. Pre-kiss intense. The bottom falls out of my stomach in the best possible way. He takes a step toward me.

"Justin!"

Connor comes around the side of the house. Justin turns in my arms towards the sound of Connor's voice. So do Brody and I, both of us taking steps backward.

My stomach feels like there's a rock in it. Brody's face has gone studiously blank.

Connor, however, isn't looking at either of us. He's beaming at Justin. "Justin, want to play peekaboo?"

And then my brother, big lug that he is, proceeds to cover his face and make improbably goofy noises at Justin.

We're joined a moment later by Clark, Easton, and Kane.

Kane is the only Wilder brother I can't quite figure out. He's just as gorgeous as his siblings—hair streaked with a hundred shades of brown and gold, pale blue eyes, and the Wilder traffic-stopping physique. But Kane has always struck me as a misfit among his energetic, adventurous brothers, more of a boy-next-door than a bear-in-the-woods type. Like he's not really a Wilder but the good looking pretty boy actor who plays one on TV.

And he always looks faintly sad to me, even more so than Clark, who lost his wife a year ago.

Kane scoops Justin out of my arms and kisses him all over his face. "Hey, buddy," he tells the baby, who is chortling with delight. His brothers join in on the Justin worship.

Gabe, too. He comes around the corner and makes a beeline for Justin.

"Jusssss!" he roars, somehow managing not to scare the crap out of the baby. He ruffles his nephew's hair.

I have to remember to tell my mother that I finally found the ultimate cure for heartbreak: watching the Wilder men make googly eyes at the world's cutest baby.

And then I look up and see the grief on Brody's face, a crack running through a beloved piece of pottery, and I forget all about that.

Rachel has Justin on her lap again. She looks like a seasoned pro, managing somehow to eat pizza and carry on a laughing conversation with Amanda and Lucy while also keeping Justin from getting ahold of her pizza and shoving it in his face. She has not, however, succeeded in preventing him from wiping pizza on her hair or her shirt.

You'd think that would be gross, but I find it charming.

I love watching Rachel with him. I love the way she murmurs to him, explaining stuff he can't possibly understand about everything that's happening. I love the way she played pat-a-cake with him earlier, holding up her own hand so he could whap his small, fat one against it. I love the way she is unconsciously bouncing one leg under him.

I know I have to tell my family about Justin not really being mine sooner rather than later. But it feels like I'll be disappointing them, too, if I take Justin away from them. It was hard to see all my brothers making a stink over him, realizing that they're going to be hurt and sad when they find out the truth.

Aside from that, having Justin here is actually great. Everyone is thrilled to see him, and they've all taken a turn with him. My mom wouldn't give him back, and insisted on being the one to give him his bottle when he got fussy and hungry.

I wanted to do it, but I knew I'd get my chance later, and I knew this would get both my mom and Amanda off my back for a while.

"My turn."

We all swivel our heads en masse in outright shock, because it's Easton who's spoken, reaching out for Justin.

Rachel hands him over, and Easton addresses Justin earnestly. "My dude," he says. "As the youngest Wilder, you have a hefty legacy to live up to."

My heart does something painful. An ungainly squeeze. Justin is not the youngest Wilder.

Sometimes I just plain wish Zoë had never told me the truth.

"Justin," Hanna says sharply. "Don't listen to that guy."

Everyone laughs.

"Justin, your Uncle Easton knows what's up."

"And that," says Hanna, "is about all Uncle Easton knows."

Easton gives Hanna a mock wounded look and goes on. "I saw you flirting with all the ladies," he tells Justin. "You've got good technique. Don't let anyone tell you otherwise."

Hanna groans and sets her pizza down. "God, Easton. You're ruining my appetite."

"Hanna," says Easton. "Nothing will ever ruin your appetite."

Some women would be offended by that. Hanna is not. She just picks up her pizza again, takes a big bite, and says, "Too true."

I STAND and head to the cooler to retrieve myself another beer. As I'm fishing for the IPA I want, Clark hurries out of the house, followed by my mother.

"I didn't mean to make you angry, Clark," she's saying.

"I'm not angry." His voice is tight.

"I just want to help."

He lifts his head, and I can see all the pain I know he's living with etched in his eyes. He just stands there for a minute. It's in his shoulders, too, the set of his jaw. Loss, misery.

We all miss her. Emma was so sweet. Good. Easy. There wasn't a mean bone in her body. She was open and generous.

I can't imagine how you'd ever replace someone like her in your heart.

"I know," Clark says finally.

My mom puts her arms around him, and he hugs her back. Then he lets her go, and she heads toward the deck, leaving me alone with Clark.

I don't ask if he's okay. I figure he has to answer that question enough.

He bends and fishes in the ice for a drink, emerging with a Corona, shaking his hand, which is bright red from the cold.

"Survival stuff doing decently?" I ask him, hoping Wilder business stuff will be a good distraction.

He shrugs.

That's about as much as anyone gets out of Clark since Emma died. He never talked much about himself—or anything—but since Emma passed away, he's even more tight-lipped. Lately, my mom and Amanda have started hassling him to get back out there and date, which I think is a mistake.

"Rachel's back, huh?"

"Yeah, so?"

"She's pretty hot."

I squint at him. Is *Clark* interested in Rachel? Something in my stomach clenches, because there is not a brother among us who would begrudge him happiness. If it had been Clark instead of Easton flirting like a fool with Lucy earlier this summer, Gabe might have given her up.

Okay, no, that *never* would have happened. But you get my point. We all want to see Clark happy so bad we'd cut off a finger for it.

"You should make a move," Clark says.

The air rushes out of my lungs, and I realize I've been holding my breath.

I don't have to choose between Clark's happiness and keeping my brother's hands off Rachel, after all.

Which is when I realize I'm fucked.

Clark takes a look at me and his eyes get wide.

"Holy shit, Brody, you and Rachel?"

I don't have to nod to confirm this; one look at my face tells him what he needs to know.

"You were actually afraid I was interested in her, huh?" He

shakes his head, and the grim line is back to his mouth, grief etched in every line of his face. "Not a fucking chance."

He looks back towards the house. "I need Mom to lay the fuck off me. Every time she starts, it's like tearing the scab off a wound."

I wince.

"I know she's just trying to help," he says.

I nod.

"But seriously, man, at this point, if I thought it would shut her up? I'd get a fake girlfriend. Let me know if you find anyone who's in the market for a pretend relationship."

I laugh like he's joking, although I'm not a hundred percent sure he is.

Also, it's not the worst idea I've ever heard.

I t takes a while for me to get Justin settled in the portacrib, but once he's down, I text Rachel. *Come over?* I give her the address.

While I'm waiting for her, I tie flies, sitting on the couch in front of my coffee table. Beads, cord, feathers, yarn, hooks, spread out in front of me, my mind blissfully empty, as it often is when I tie.

This is my meditation, right here. One beaded nymph after another, while the sedges and midges I've already finished form small, neat, satisfying piles.

Tying flies also brings my father back to me, because fly fishing was something I usually did alone with him. Gabe never loved fishing the way I did. He liked hunting better. So when my dad and I went together, there was no Gabe to upstage or one-up me. There was just the river, the line, the fly, the fish—and me and my dad.

Wrap, wrap, wrap, wrap.

Rap, rap, rap.

When I open the door, she's standing there, absolutely beautiful with her hair down and her *I'm here if it's no trouble* smile. I want to pull her into my arms and make love to her all night. Fuck telling her this story. Fuck everything except the way she makes me feel. Instead, I hold the door open, and she steps inside.

She looks around my apartment, and smiles. "This is very you."

My eyes follow hers, trying to see what she sees. I keep it simple: a comfortable couch, an equally comfortable recliner, a flat screen TV, a coffee table.

She steps to the wall, looking at the framed posters hanging there. One for *A River Runs Through It*, the 1992 movie that my dad made me watch as a kid for the fly fishing. If she's ever seen it, it's probably because someone told her Brad Pitt was hot in it.

She stops in front of my three national parks posters, side by side—Yellowstone, Zion, and Olympic National Park. "These are beautiful. My parents aren't much for the outdoors, so I haven't been to many parks."

"We'll have to fix that," I say, before I can think better of it. Because who knows if Rachel and I will ever hang out together again once her visit home is over.

One of my hands closes into a fist.

"I'd like that," she says, shyly, and I can't decide if that makes it better or worse.

Just more confusing, maybe.

She runs her hands across the spines of the few books on my small shelf. Mostly mysteries and thrillers. "Loved this one," she says, pointing to Tana French's *In the Woods*.

"Me too."

"I didn't know you liked to read."

"I'm slow," I admit. "But I don't mind when it's not for school. When no one's riding my ass about it." I shrug. "Fly fishing's slow, too. I like slow."

She smiles in a way that makes me picture kissing her, leisurely and languid, while I move in her. Maybe she's picturing it, too, because her cheeks pink up.

But before I can take a step towards her, she says, "Justin's so cute."

Right. We have things to talk about.

I offer her a seat on my couch and a cold beer. She settles on the couch but says she just wants water—"I drank way too much beer already today."

We sit for a moment in awkward silence. And there's no good segue, so I just jam the throttle: "Rachel. He's not mine."

Her mouth falls open.

"That's why I said not to believe everything you hear."

"But—you were—going to marry his mother?"

"I thought he was mine. I had no clue he wasn't. God. I don't know where to start."

"Start at the beginning."

That makes me laugh. She makes it sound so goddamn easy, but what is the beginning?

The night I hooked up with Zoë for the first time? The night the condom—from her stash—broke before I'd filled it? The day she told me she was pregnant and it was mine? Or the day Connor told me he'd seen her with someone else?

None of those, actually. The beginning of the end was the day I looked down into my son's eyes and saw the truth.

"When Zoë told me she was pregnant, I was totally freaked out. But once I got used to the idea, I didn't hate it. And I started manning up. I registered for a program to get my GED. I buckled down and started turning things around, doing more around the office, taking the business more seriously. I vowed not to fuck up with Gabe anymore. So I could be a good dad and a good husband. And then..."

I stop. My stomach flips, just like it did that day.

"I was in the middle of the fucking GED course. We were doing the genetics unit. The part where they use eye color to explain how genes are recessive or dominant, you know?

"I went home and I picked him up. He dangled there, kicking his little feet and grinning at me. And his eyes were brown.

"I mean, they'd been basically brown since he was born. Kind of a muddy color. Everyone kept saying they'd get lighter, but they didn't. They were getting browner."

She stares at me.

"Zoë has green eyes. I have green eyes." I cross my arms. "And there it was, right in front of me. Justin's eyes should be either green or blue."

"Brody, I—"

"I asked Zoë about it. She probably could have bullshitted me. I think I wanted to be bullshitted. But I think she needed it off her chest. I think the lie was killing her. And she just kind of folded. Confessed everything. Two-timing both me and Len, getting pregnant, figuring out it had to be him. He's married—to someone else—so the path of least resistance for her was to keep the whole thing with Len a secret, let me believe I was Justin's dad, and put my name on his birth certificate."

"Oh, Brody." Her eyes are so tender. "I can't even..."

I wish she'd stop looking at me like that, because it's making me feel all the things I haven't let myself feel, except in the smallest fits and starts.

"I got a DNA test, and, yeah, he's not mine. So I left. Moved out. Quit the GED course. Starting missing work again, calling in sick, bailing out on charters, like nothing had changed. Like Justin had never been—"

I cut myself off before my voice can break.

"Brody."

I wave her off. "It's okay, Rachel."

She shakes her head. "It's not okay."

"But what am I supposed to do about it?" I ask, with a bitter laugh. "I have to let it go."

"It's so unfair." Outrage tightens her voice. "You were trying so hard to be a better person, and you got punished for it."

"Yeah, well, that's how it goes sometimes."

She looks away, staring at the *River Runs Through It* poster blankly. Then turns back.

"Connor knows?"

I nod. "He's the only one who knows the whole story. Connor's always had faith in me, even when pretty much no one else did. From the minute I dropped out he tried to convince me to get my GED. He was convinced if I did, I could join him at college. He tried so hard to talk me into it. I kept telling him I didn't have what it took, and he kept telling me I was full of it."

"And with your dad gone and your mom so sick when you were in high school, it probably felt like no one at home cared."

"Gabe was taking care of my mom and trying to save the business. And I was the fuckup who made it harder on both of them. I can't tell you how many times one of them had to bail me out of my own shit."

Her face darkens. "You were a hurting fourteen-year-old boy. What teenager who'd just lost his dad wouldn't be a mess?"

She says it so vehemently, I almost believe it. But then I remember my dad asking Gabe to run the business and take care of the family. Gabe asking Clark to run the business if he had to move to Boston.

Zoë saying she and Justin would be better off with Len after he left his wife because he was a hardworking guy with a real job.

"I get it," Rachel says quietly. "Why you value your friendship with Connor so much. If he's the one guy who's ever seen you for the man you really are."

It feels like she's smacked me in the middle of the chest. In a good way, but also—it hurts.

"And I understand if you don't feel like you can, um, do this," she says. She makes a gesture that loops in both of us. "I haven't been fair, asking you to go behind Connor's back and risk that friendship."

I watch her quietly. The way her eyes take me in. Seeing me.

The man you really are.

I have to close my eyes for a second. When I open them again, she's still looking at me. And I make a decision.

I cross my arms. "Being with you *does* put my friendship with Connor at risk."

Her shoulders slump. She straightens right away, but I see it. And that gives me even more courage. She wants this, too.

"But to loosely quote an amazing woman I know—" I reach behind her and gently tug the elastic out of her hair so I can thread my fingers through it— "I don't fucking care."

I lean in and kiss her.

When Amanda first sends out the invitations for girls' night, it's at her house, but at the last minute she emails everyone—including me— to change the venue to Rush Creek Bakery. No explanation. I mean, not that she needs one. Nan's baked goods have been a Rush Creek treat since before I was born. I'm not surprised when she pulls a tray of hot chocolate chip cookies out of the oven just for us.

But once the vibrators have made their appearance and we're passing them around, Amanda explains herself.

"You guys know from the e-vite that it was originally supposed to be at my house?"

Lots of nods. Hanna's here, and Lucy, along with a passel of Amanda's other friends, mostly youngish moms who keep making not-exactly-jokes about how long it's been since they had sex and how unlikely it is that that will change any time soon.

"Two days ago, I found out Heath had to work late. And I just kept picturing one of the kids waking up or not being able to sleep and running down the stairs and popping into the living room while there were toys spread out everywhere. And how would I explain this?"

She holds up one of the most popular toys, a rabbit vibrator. This is the original—like the one Miranda famously hips Charlotte to on *Sex and the City*. On this model, the part that juts out to provide clitoral stimulation looks like an actual bunny, even though the more modern rabbit designs only vaguely hint at floppy ears and hopping.

Amanda brandishes the rabbit. "One of the kids would totally grab it and be like, Mommy! It's a bunny! How does it work? Oh, look, it's a vibrating bunny! Can I take it to school for show and tell? Is it a kid toy? It has beads inside!" She bounces up and down, mimicking kid excitement, then drops abruptly back to adult tones. "I was like, no *way* we're doing this at my house."

Laughter bounces around the circle, and the moms all echo their fervent agreement. And then the stories start to fly.

"I've got one for you. My fifteen-year-old, who has gotten very self-sufficient lately and doesn't usually want anything to do with me, came into the bedroom about a month ago when I was reading in bed, threw himself down on the floor next to the bed and started chatting with me about life, school, and everything. And then after we've been talking for a few minutes, he gets this weird look on his face, reaches under the bed, surfaces with my Magic Wand in hand, and says, 'What's this?' And instead of being all cool and saying, 'Oh, that's a muscle massager,' or using it as an opportunity to talk about masturbation and toys, I freak out and yell, '*Put that down!*' He drops it like a hot potato. And obviously, that was the last mother-son bonding time we've had since. I'm still mad at myself."

Murmurs of sympathy.

"Yeah, so, under the bed? Not the best hiding place."

"Have to agree with that—my We-Vibe charging cable got mangled in the vacuum. While it was being run under the bed by our cleaning service. I came home to find it on my bed: vibe, mangled cord, apology note."

"Did they come back? The cleaning crew?"

"Yeah. And I've never been able to be home when they have, since. I can't face them."

Laughter.

"Have you ever been walked in on?"

A moment of silence, and then a burst of simultaneous starts:

"Oh, my God, I have to tell you—"

"Oh, it was the worst, the *worst!*"

Amanda's friend Susie:

"We were doing it in the bathroom because the door locks, except we were so sleep deprived that my wife unlocked the door instead of locking it, and my three-year-old walked in."

Peals of laughter.

Kiona: "We were in bed in the dark, and I started to get that 'you're being watched' feeling and I realized my four-year-old was standing by the side of the bed. Literally *no* idea how long he'd been there."

Groans of dismay.

Jem: "They're all going to end up in the therapy for all the ways we messed them up anyway, right?"

Whole-hearted agreement.

"What about you, Amanda, any horror stories?"

For whatever reason, my eyes happen to be on Amanda's face when the question gets asked, so I can see her expression change. It goes studiously blank, a blankness I recognize because I saw a version of it on Brody's face the other day when the subject of Justin came up. It's Wilder for, "There be dragons."

Then she smiles, an easy, practiced social smile. "You'd have to actually *have* sex to get walked in on, wouldn't you? Double income, two workaholics, three kids under ten, you do the math," Amanda says, with a shrug.

She gets more laughter and a round of amens, and the "easy" smile stays on her face, but she's not fooling me.

And she's not fooling Lucy, who's watching her friend and frowning.

Huh, I think. And Amanda's life seems so perfect.

Perfect.

There's that word again.

"Hey."

Gabe stands a few feet away from the trailered small boat, leaning against a tree, his dog Buck at his side. I've just finished checking the plugs and fuel filter. It's deja vu from our fight over the reviews.

He climbs up beside me. "You want some help?"

Startled, I say, "Sure."

That's how Gabe and I come to be working side by side, me quietly checking the fuses and wiring while he hooks up the trickle charger. Buck noses around the inside of the boat, hopping down from time to time, then back up again.

I catch myself humming. Humming!

I'm not a guy who hums when he works.

Or ever.

But I'm in such a good mood.

Getting some will do that to a guy, I tell myself, but I know it's more than that. First of all, Rachel and I still haven't officially had the kind of sex that involves me burying myself balls deep in her—

Gah.

But we have been spending a lot of time together the last week and a half, since the night when I told her what happened with Zoë and Justin. We've done a couple of parties, but we've also spent time talking and kissing and making each other feel really, really good. Telling her about Justin changed things between us. Some of it was the relief of telling someone. Anyone. But some of it was how carefully she listened. And what she said afterwards.

I get it. Why you value your friendship with Connor so much. If he's the one guy who's ever seen you for the man you really are.

Gabe clears his throat, drawing my eyes up from where I'm working. "I just wanted to say I appreciate the money you've been bringing in."

I try not to keel over from sheer shock. Even when I was trying to turn over a new leaf with Gabe, when Zoë was first pregnant with Justin, he never outright praised me.

I almost tell him that, but then I think better of it. "Thanks."

"Can I ask a question?"

My normal response: *You're going to do it anyway, so is there really any point to your asking me?*

But today I say, "Sure."

Gabe's eyebrows go up. He wasn't expecting that. He was expecting the usual snark from me.

"All the money coming in from you. That's not all Real Romance parties, is it?"

It's not really a question.

I never told Gabe about my plan, and I never updated Lucy on where it stood.

"No," I say. "Not all Real Romance."

I tell him about the new parties with my game store, book store, and spa partners. I explain that I started doing the sessions... and they've been working. The partners and I are making money. The clients—mostly women, but sometimes also couples—love them.

And best of all, I've been upselling the other trips at the end of each session, and getting signups.

Gabe nods. "I wondered where the random new signups were coming from. There were a bunch we couldn't account for from any other funnel."

I nod.

"I need you to keep me in the loop," Gabe says in his boss/dad/asshole voice.

Two weeks ago, that would have sent me to the moon on a rage-rocket. But for whatever reason, today, I get it.

I've been a pain in Gabe's ass. As a kid, I made him pick me up, staggering drunk or stoned out of my mind, from parties all over the Five Rivers region. He had to phone in my fake school excuses, show up at the principal's office to pick me up for suspensions. He called my employers to beg them to give me back jobs I'd done everything I could to lose. He bailed me out of the drunk tank, cleaned me up after fights, gave me work when I couldn't—or really, more accurately, wouldn't—hold down another job.

And when he did, I rewarded him by bucking his authority, snarking at him, and generally giving him shit.

Since Zoë got pregnant, the only truly hotheaded thing I've done was throw a punch at Len, and I had plenty of good reasons to do that.

But Gabe doesn't know that.

So it makes sense that he'd still have a few doubts.

And for once, I feel like it's my job to close the gap.

"For real, Gabe. You can trust me."

I don't think I've ever said anything like that to my brother. Usually it would be, *What the fuck? You don't trust me?*

I'm not sure how he's going to react.

My heart's beating like it does when Zoë calls. Or when Rachel gets anywhere in a hundred-foot radius.

Maybe that's a bad example, only because it's the least of my reactions to Rachel being near.

But you get the gist.

Gabe's stern gaze assesses me for so long, I want to take back what I said about trusting me. And then he blows out a breath and says:

"Okay."

Okay. And that's it. That's the end of the conversation.

After all that—after all these years—he's willing to do it. To trust me.

Maybe it's Lucy's influence on him.

Or maybe things are changing for me.

I've worked really hard these last few weeks, and I haven't minded or resented it.

Even before Rachel said those words—*the man you really are*—I wanted to be that man for her.

So maybe it's that. Gabe's softer, and I'm—invested.

But it's also possible that I missed the truth, which is that at any point, if I'd asked Gabe nicely to trust me...?

He would have been willing to do it.

I open my mouth to ask, but there's a strange—choking—noise from behind me, on the boat.

Gabe moves so fast he's almost a blur, grabbing Buck and practically tossing him out of the boat, depositing him on the ground below. And not a moment too soon, because Buck proceeds to lose the contents of his stomach in the grass.

Gabe groans, then leans over. "Why is Buck's vomit purple and glittery?"

It takes me a minute, but I figure it out. "We did a small party in this boat, and I guess one of Rachel's toys got left behind. Buck must have found it and chewed it up."

"God damn," Gabe says. "I'm going to have to call the vet and make sure silicone isn't toxic to dogs."

"That one's latex," I tell him.

Gabe shoots me a long, hard look.

"What? I have nothing to do but listen to her spiel."

And watch her handle the merch.

My cock gets heavy, thinking about it.

Gabe's eyes narrow. Then narrow more.

"What?!" I'm already defending myself.

"You tell me!"

I'm about to lie by omission, or at least quibble by omission, but then Gabe says, "If you're not sleeping with her yet, you're going to."

"What the fuck are you talking about?"

I frown at him, but only so I don't smile. And is that a smile I see on my brother's face?

No fucking way.

"You know how I know that?" Gabe asks.

I shake my head.

"Buck has put his stamp of approval on it."

My brother is talking straight up nonsense. "You're joking, right?"

"No. I'm dead serious." And then Gabe tells me a story. About the boat ride I took Lucy on earlier this summer, her unfortunate seasickness incident, and the fate of one of his sweatshirts.

"So," Gabe concludes. "Buck is putting his stamp of approval on you and Rachel."

I open my mouth to tell Gabe that he's not making any sense, but then I stop. Because I realize what Gabe is saying, in his own, roundabout way.

Gabe approves.

And that's twice in one day, so there's no fucking way I'm going to argue with him.

26

RACHEL

"Rachel," my mom says. "Brody Wilder is on a motorcycle outside. You're not going on his bike, are you?"

Concern laces her voice. Her eyebrows bend together in a V.

I look out the window.

My mom's right. Brody's shiny, beautiful black motorcycle sits in the driveway, but that's not where my eyes are. They are on Brody, pulling his helmet off and shaking out his rumpled hair. On his thighs, braced around the steel and fiberglass frame. On his leather boots and torn jeans, and his big hands, the leather cuffs on his wrists, the ink on his arms.

I look at my mother, and think about all the times I sat up with her at night while she waited for Connor to come home, and how I vowed never to be the kid who caused her worry.

She will worry about me the whole time I'm gone, if I get on that bike with Brody.

In general, making people worry is one of the many things I pride myself on not doing.

She's totally justified, too, because motorcycles are dangerous. Getting on that bike has not ever been and will never be part of any sane, well-thought through plan.

And you know what?

I'm going to do it anyway.

Being her good girl, being *anyone's* good girl, doing it right, getting it perfect?

They're all old habits I can give up now.

"I don't want to stress you out," I tell her. "But I think if I don't do this? I might regret it for the rest of my life."

Something like a smile smooths out the wrinkles in my mother's forehead.

"Oh," she says. "It's like that, is it?"

I nod. "Yeah. It's like that."

She nods. "Well. Yes. I'll worry about you the whole time you're gone. But all of parenthood is about trying to figure out the balance between tying your children to your waist and letting them run around in the world. All right. I'll try to find a new show to watch on Netflix so I won't think about it too much. But he better have a second helmet."

I can see him out there, holding it. "He does."

I give her a big hug, and I promise her we'll go slow and stay on familiar roads, even though I have no idea if that's true.

"You might..." I take a deep breath. "Not want to mention this to Connor. If you feel like you can omit it without, I don't know, lying."

My mother smiles. "Poor Connor. No one wants to tell him anything."

"If he weren't so dang opinionated, maybe we'd tell him more stuff."

"I might be able to fail to mention it. But you might want to think about telling him that you and Brody—" She looks outside. "—are?" she finishes. A question.

I shake my head. "Does it make any sense to tell him when I'll be gone in a week, two at most?"

She tilts her head to the side. "You're sure about that?"

I don't answer her, because I don't know the answer.

"I've always liked Brody Wilder," she says. "He has good manners and a big heart. I figured he'd get the rest of it out of his system."

I don't want Brody Wilder to get anything out of his system. I like him exactly the way he is.

I don't say that out loud, but maybe my mom can see it on my face, because she says, "Oh, Rachel."

I give her one more hug. Then I step outside and wave at the beautiful man on the beautiful bike in my parents' driveway.

He waves back, and a smile breaks over his face, lighting up the world.

Okay, Brody Wilder, you got me, I think.

He hands me the helmet, shows me how to fasten the chinstrap, and tests it to make sure it fits.

"You'll mount behind me, here," he says. "There's no backrest, so you have to hang on to me tight."

"Mount behind you. Hold on tight. Sounds pretty good to me."

Brody's eyes get big.

I grin. "What? Did you think good girls didn't talk dirty?"

"Pleasantly surprised," he murmurs. "If you need to tell me something while we're riding, you can tap my shoulder once for 'stop when it's convenient,' twice for 'it's urgent,' and three times for 'right the fuck now.'" His gaze flicks to mine and I raise my eyebrows.

"Are there signals for slower and faster, too?" I ask.

He closes his eyes. "Rachel."

"Just curious."

"Pat my right thigh for slower," he says. "And if you want to go faster? Squeeze me tight with your thighs."

He delivers that instruction with full-on Brody smolder and my knees go liquid. Pretty sure he's messing with me on that one, but I'm okay with it.

He gives me a few more instructions—what not to touch, because it's hot, what to do when we're turning, how *not* to throw him off balance, and how I'll get off the bike at the end.

I throw a leg over, the way he showed me, settle my feet in the footrests, according to his instructions, grab him tight with my thighs, and wrap my arms around his waist.

Which, oh, my God is so hard. Brody Wilder is all muscle. How does my body know that the feel of his abs under my hands is a signal to start melting?

I hope I don't lose all control and start groping him midway through the ride.

And then we're upright and he kicks the bike into motion and holy wowser.

I wasn't expecting it to be so noisy or so—

Buzzy between my thighs.

And even with the helmet on and no way for the wind to slip fingers through my hair, the speed and the rushing of air is a total thrill.

Not to mention the man between my thighs and in my arms.

My whole body burns at the contact.

He takes us on a long, slow cruise around Rush Creek. I notice, though, that he avoids the area near Connor's apartment and town itself.

It's impossible to ignore the roar of the engine or the vibrations that surge through the powerful machine. But it's also impossible for me to ignore what those vibrations, in combination with Brody's hard body, do to me.

I'm vibrating, too, by the time he takes the bike down a long, dirt road that emerges into a grassy meadow.

"Brody," I say, when it's quiet enough for me to be heard. My arms are still around his waist. "Nobody told me a motorcycle was a sex toy."

His chuckle is burnt vanilla, rough like his stubble on my thighs that day at the lake.

I am all heat and liquid and craving.

He half turns, carefully avoiding the hot pipe, and lifts me onto his lap. He removes my helmet, and his, and leans down to drop them into the grass. Then he kisses me. No preliminaries, just hot, open mouth and searching tongue, leaving tingles everywhere it sweeps. When he pulls away, I'm panting.

"You all revved up?" he murmurs.

"God. Yes."

"Hold on tight."

I lock my arms around his neck, and in a feat of athleticism that takes my breath away, he stands, swings his leg off the bike, and—without putting me down—works open the strap of his motorcycle satchel to remove a blanket. He sets me down to lay it out, then swoops me up again. A moment later, we're on the ground, his body covering mine.

Brody Wilder is better than my teenaged fantasies, which is—

Well, off the charts.

Actually, this scene bears a *striking* resemblance to my teenaged fantasies. The way he's kissing me, like he can't get enough. The weight of his hips exactly where I want it. And Brody Wilder knows how to move. A hitch, a swivel, the perfect amount of friction through his jeans and mine.

I pant and writhe under him, lifting my hips to try to get more contact. He kisses me deeper, slides a hand between us and into the V of my thighs. Working me with his palm, getting the pressure in exactly the right place. He breaks the kiss long enough to ask, "Like this?" and I nod. He wedges his thigh where his hand was, working the thick, denim-clad muscle over the damp seam of my jeans. I am already on the edge, and he somehow knows exactly how much pressure I need and want. The pleasure is both amplified and muted by the layers between us.

He finds my nipple through my t-shirt and bra, brushing his thumb back and forth over it.

"Brody," I beg, but he just kisses me again.

He's relentless, the thumb on my nipple, the rhythm and friction of his thigh, and I try to slow him down, to draw it out, but he breaks the kiss, watching me, eyes gone dark at whatever he sees in my face. I'm helpless, and he holds my gaze, eyes green and fierce on my face, knowing exactly what he's doing to me.

"Brody!"

"That's it, you come, baby. Come for me."

I'm clutching him, thrusting up desperately to meet him, coming in thick, drowning waves of pleasure.

He cups his hand over my throbbing mound, feeling me through the last surges and aftershocks, his expression... awestruck.

"Holy fucking God, Rachel, you're so hot. If I had had the slightest idea, high school would have been an entirely different experience for both of us."

"Probably for the best," I manage, breathless. "Want me to—?"

He lets me unfasten him, and then I kneel and take him in my fist, ducking my head to lick around the tip of his cock.

"If you don't want me to come in your mouth, you should probably know that I'm pretty worked up."

His hands are tangling in my hair. Gently, though. No force, no pressure. It feels good.

"It's okay," I say, and take him in my mouth. I love the sensation, the velvet of the taut head, the way each suck I give him echoes in my core. I pop off and say, "I'm not, like, good with the whole, you know, *deep* thing."

"You don't have to prove anything to me. You don't have to take me deep and you don't have to swallow. It's only sexy if you like it."

Brody Wilder has destroyed me for all men, I think, as I resume licking and sucking him, loving it in a way I have never loved a blow job before. Genuinely. Wanting to make him feel good the way *I* do and not the way some nameless faceless sex goddess might.

And I think I do all right, because a moment later he's calling my name, pulling my hair (still feels so damn good), and coming (in my mouth).

And I love it the whole time.

"Rachel," he says, much more quietly, when he's done. "Ahhh. Thank you."

"You don't have to thank me. It was good for me."

He laughs quietly, that rough honey chuckle. "I can't unlearn my manners."

"I wouldn't want you to."

When he can stand again, he extracts two cans of root beer and a paper sack bearing the Rush Creek Bakery logo from his motorcycle bag.

"Picnic time." He spreads the blanket and we sit. The sky is blue, the sun is warm, and it's that magic time of year and day when the whole world holds still except for the hum and buzz of insects among the wildflowers in the field.

The paper sack holds Nan's cookies.

"Oh, you are my hero."

"That's all it takes?"

I nod.

"This is my perfect date," Brody says. He says it super casually, but I feel like it contains a world of significance.

"Motorcycle ride and picnic?"

He nods.

"It's pretty dang great."

He smiles, maybe at my inadequate curse.

"What about fishing? I would have thought that would be your dream date."

"I mean, that would be pretty amazing, too. But there aren't a lot of women who want to go fishing as a date." He thinks about it. "Actually, zero. There are zero women I know who'd want to go fishing as a date."

"I'd go."

"Yeah? For real?"

"Sure."

"Monday?"

He sounds so eager, it makes me laugh. But only kind of. The other part of me feels like some shy wild creature has just eaten out of my hand. "Absolutely."

I wake up way too early on Monday morning, wishing I hadn't asked Rachel to go fly fishing.

Because here's the thing: I really like Rachel. And I love fly fishing.

But some things that are great on their own aren't meant to be blended. Split pea soup with smoked bacon, and mint chocolate chip ice cream, for example. Separately? Brilliant. Together? Scary.

Most people are too impatient for fly fishing. Too chatty. Too inquisitive. I'm careful who I take on my river charters, because I don't want to ruin fly fishing for myself.

I pick up Rachel in the truck.

She ambles down the front steps, and she's fucking adorable—wearing a baseball cap and a fishing vest, carrying waders and a pair of wading boots. Since I know Connor didn't outfit her, I'm guessing she asked for help from Amanda, Hanna, and Lucy. Between the three of them they probably have all the gear, but if not, they know who to ask.

The vest is huge. It might be her dad's. She's swimming in its hugeness.

Under the adorable?

She's fucking sexy. The fishing vest hangs open, and she's wearing a thin lavender base layer underneath that clings to her curves. It makes me want to bail out on the whole trip right now and just undress her.

She sees me staring at her and raises her eyebrows. "Did I do okay?"

I nod. "You look great. And you make that shit look hot."

Her smile lights up the early-morning Perez property.

She climbs into the truck.

"Do you want music?" I ask, pulling out of the driveway.

"Um, do you mind if we don't? Sometimes I just really like it quiet."

You can't always know what you crave until it lands in your lap. I don't think I could have predicted that Rachel's simple observation would feel like a gift. But here we are, headed out to the upper Mionet River, the windows cracked, the radio silent, the sun still fighting to clear the morning mist, and it's so goddamn peaceful.

And she's part of the peace, like she soaks up some of the ambient noise.

I reach out and take her hand, and she squeezes mine back.

I show her how to cast. How the line floats out first, and the fly follows. I tell her that if you do it right, it's called bending and stroking the rod.

"You're making that up."

"I'm not."

She shakes her head. "Lucy should redo all her marketing campaigns just to focus on all the hotness the Wilder Brothers generate in a normal day. Sex sells, right?"

"I guess it does." I dip down to kiss her neck, soft as silk. "You're going to sunburn here."

"Damn. I forgot sunscreen."

"It's OK." I produce an extra neck gaiter from my pocket.

"Seriously, you just carry gear like this around?"

"Guys who run charters get used to bailing people out. Also, I'm not as good at it as I seem."

I tell her the story of the first totally inauspicious book club. The missing TP, bug wipes, and sunscreen. The women and their gossip. Chicklet's unintended swimming lesson. My reviews.

She makes faces and frowns and laughs in all the right places, and it takes the sting out of the memory.

"I wondered why you issued individual portions on the TP. And what accounted for that very intense sign in the head about menstrual products going in the provided trash bag."

"Now you know," I say. "Extreme trauma relating to having to snake *and* pump out the head."

She laughs and takes another—not very successful—shot at casting.

But before too long, she gets the hang of it, and we stand side by side—as close as we can without risking tangling— and cast into the lazy Mionet.

She's quiet for a long time, and I can't tell you how much I appreciate it. Standing with her, enjoying the rush of the river, the calls of crows and eagles. The songs of smaller birds.

The sight of her, standing quietly, patiently, waiting with me.

I had no idea how much I wanted this. None.

LATER IN THE MORNING, as the cooler gets heavier with trout and the birds quiet down for midday, we both get chattier. I explain to her a bunch about the different kinds of lures.

"What's the one you keep in your pocket?" she asks.

I hadn't known she'd noticed.

"My dad and I made it when I was little. I loved it and wanted to keep it with me instead of putting it in the tackle box. So he cut the hook off, and I've had it ever since. It's kind of a good-luck charm. Or worry stone. Both."

She smiles at that. "Your dad was always so nice to me. I miss him."

"Me too."

She nods.

"Are you going to teach Justin? To fish?"

I feel myself freeze, and I see the moment where she picks up on it.

"I'm sorry," she says, quickly. "That was—the wrong question." Then she takes a deep breath. "It's just—it's so clear how much you love him. Maybe you should try to spend more time with him. If his parents are okay with that."

The suggestion doesn't hurt as much as I would have expected it to. It feels...okay. "Zoë asked me to. To spend more time with him. She needs more childcare now that Len went back to his wife."

She winces.

"Yeah."

"Once a dick, always a dick." She sighs. "I wish I could warn Werner's next girlfriend."

"Did you just curse?"

She smiles. "I think I did. I mean, call a dick a dick, right?"

I grin.

"Maybe Justin would like going out on the boat. He's old enough now to get the wind and the sky and the water, right?"

"I don't know," I say.

"Pretty sure he knows a lot more about what's going on than we think. We should take him out."

We.

I try not to love the sound of that, and fail.

"When I was his dad—"

I choke on the words.

"Brody."

She can't set down the rod or approach me without tangling us, but she reaches out a hand, and I take it. Her touch calms me enough that I can get the rest of the sentence out. "That was my fantasy. That I'd teach him about the boat. Teach him to be an angler. A fly fisherman."

"You don't have to lose that part," she says. "You still can."

I let the thought sit for a moment. I let myself picture it again.

It feels good.

I squeeze her hand.

Then I say, "The wedding was supposed to be a week from Saturday."

"How are you feeling about that?" she asks, cautiously.

I test myself out around it. Poke the date and the event, Zoë and Justin and Len, with the edges of my bruised emotions.

I squeeze her hand again.

"Surprisingly okay."

I'm rewarded with a Rachel smile so big it hurts my chest.

"Look, Justin! Elk!"

I point to the shore, and his baby gaze seems to follow mine, but it's hard to tell. I don't know how far a six-month-old can see, how sharp his vision is at picking out the large, brown deer-like creature from the rest of the woods, or whether he cares. He grabs my finger and babbles, so that seems like a good start.

Justin, Brody, and I are out on Brody's small fishing boat on one of the lakes in the national forest, soaking up some mid-summer sunshine and each other's company, and, man, this is the life. After I suggested to Brody that he try to spend more time with Justin, he told Zoë he wanted to take Justin out in the boat, and she said it was fine, as long as he wore a life jacket. So he's twice as roly-poly in one of those little baby life vests.

I carry Justin back to where Brody is casually piloting the boat and wearing yet another form-fitting t-shirt and pair of butt-flattering ripped jeans. I let myself enjoy the ink-and-ropy-muscle forearm porn for a moment, until Justin squawks and reaches for Brody. I tip the baby into Brody's arms.

Gah, the two of them. Squishy baby and ripped dad. I allow myself the luxury of ogling. And enjoy the melting sensation in my chest.

Brody steers us to a spot that's shaded by the angle of sun and mountain, and we drift a bit. Brody takes advantage of the opportunity to let Justin "steer." He plants Justin's fat little hands on the wheel, and Justin appears delighted, slapping his palms repeatedly on the wheel and turning to give his father a gummy grin.

"You're so good with him," I say.

"I don't know about that."

Brody's scowling, something I realize I haven't seen him do in quite a while.

"Hey," I say. "I'm sorry if that was the wrong thing to say."

"What makes you think that?"

I raise my eyebrows. "Your scowl."

"I'm not scowling."

All I can do is laugh. For a second, Brody's scowl deepens, then breaks. Not quite a smile, but the corner of his mouth quirks. It makes me feel like I've been crowned queen of all I survey.

Justin reaches up and grabs Brody's mouth.

"Ow," Brody says. "Dude, that hurts. Save the hooks for the fish." He untangles Justin's fingers from his lower lip. Justin puts both his baby hands on the sides of Brody's face and smacks his forehead into Brody's chin.

"Why?" Brody demands, lifting Justin up so they're face-to-face. "Why do you want to hurt me, little man?"

Justin chortles and drools on Brody's face.

"Oh, God," Brody says. "You need a new diaper."

He grabs the diaper bag, plops Brody down on a mat on one of the benches in the stern, and proceeds to execute a surprisingly speedy and hazard-free change. It's been years since I babysat, and I was never an expert, but I can recognize true skill when I see it.

There's something ridiculously hot about a tattooed biker bad boy changing a diaper without batting an eyelash.

He gets Justin dressed again, lets him lie on the seat, kicking his legs. He finds a bright colored toy with a million dangly bits and hands it to Justin, who alternates between shoving it in his mouth and hooting at the sky.

We both watch him, because babies. They're full-time entertainment.

"Do you want kids?" I ask Brody.

He nods. "I didn't think I did. And then this guy came along. So yeah, I do, but..."

He stops.

"What?"

He shrugs, and pulls the lure—the one from his dad—out of his pocket. Fidgets with it. I know him well enough by now to know it means something big's bugging him.

He worries the body of the "fly" with his thumb, then sighs. "I don't know if I've got what it takes."

"What do you mean?"

"I got a taste of how much responsibility there is. And I guess I just don't know if I'm the guy who signs up for that."

"I think you could be. If you wanted to be."

"Yeah," he says.

I wait for him to say something else, but he doesn't. He's

scowling again, and worrying the lure, and I don't want to press.

"Hey," he says, a moment later. "What about you? I've gotten to go on *three* of my favorite dates now: a motorcycle ride, a river fishing expedition, and a day on the boat. What about yours? What's your dream date?"

I have to think about it a minute. "This is pretty great," I admit, surveying the gorgeous scene around us. "But I think my favorite would be if someone ever cooked for me."

"If someone *ever* cooked for you," he repeats. "Does that mean no one has ever cooked for you?"

I think about this, hard, and conclude: "I mean, my parents and my grandparents, of course. But no guy, no."

"Your ex must have, though. You lived together, right?"

I shake my head, finally able to admit to myself that Werner was a straight up …

I abandon the attempt to find a non-filthy way to characterize Werner. He was an asshole, pure and simple. "He cooked for me if you count eggs and mac and cheese. And takeout pizza. Also, he made me cold cereal right before he cheated on me."

Brody's eyes narrow, and his jaw ticks. "Can I just repeat that your ex is a criminally shitty human being?"

"As many times as you'd like."

He squints into the sun, then smiles at me. My body temperature rises a hundred and fifty degrees.

"So here's how it's going to go," he says. "We're going to drop Justin off with Zoë, head back to my place, and I'll cook you dinner."

"You cook?" I ask, although if the bad boy changes diapers, why am I surprised that he also cooks?

"Just one of my many, many skills," he says, eyes all sexy intent. "Wait till you experience all the things I'm good at."

Okay, maybe I'm not so much surprised as struck dumb by the embarrassment of riches that is Brody Wilder.

And a little bit terrified, because I'm pretty sure that I'm falling for the bad boy.

We drop off Justin first. Rachel waits in the truck while I walk Justin up to the door.

"How'd it go?" Zoë asks, taking him from me. He fusses a little and clings to my shirt. I have to admit, it makes me feel like a superhero, even though I feel sad for Justin, too. I wish Zoë had found a way to give him a life where all the people he loves were in one place. That's not the way it is, though.

But I can make sure Justin always knows he's loved. I can do that.

"I want to see him more," I tell her. "I'll take him whenever you need me to and I can. I want him to know I'm in his life."

Zoë nods, like she's been expecting this. "I want to take a girls' trip to California next month. Would you want to do four days then?"

"Email me the dates, and if I can work it around my trips or get a couple of hours of childcare from my family, I'm in."

She beams. "Thank you. I know you don't have to do this, but I appreciate it."

"I'm not doing it for you." I don't say it angrily. Just honestly. "I'm doing it for Justin."

"I know."

We share a weak smile. This is probably the best place we'll ever get to, and I'm suddenly glad we're here.

And grateful to Rachel for helping me get here.

"Bye, little dude," I tell Justin, who has quit being mad about my leaving and buried his face in his mom's shirt. That was quick. Luckily, babies are resilient.

Back at the truck, I say, "thank you," to Rachel.

"What for?"

"For making me do the right thing by Justin instead of sulking about how Zoë screwed me over. I still wish Justin were mine, but I'd rather be his fun uncle than no one in his life."

She smiles at me. "You're a really good fun uncle."

I think of what she said earlier, that I would make a good father. When she said it, I let myself, for a split second, imagine a different scene. The two of us, on a boat, with a child. Our child. And then I pushed it out of my head.

I start the truck. "I'm going to take a spin by the farmer's market and pick up a few things for dinner."

"Can we make a stop first? By my house? There are a few things I want to grab. If you're doing dinner, I want to be in charge of dessert."

"Sure."

We make a quick run by the Perez homestead, and she emerges with a plastic shopping bag from Rush to Read Books, which she tucks into the side map pocket.

I eye the bag. "You're not going to tell me what you're making?"

She shakes her head. "I'm just going to say that I know you'll like it."

"Okay."

We stop by the farmer's market and I grab a bottle of local wine, a six-pack of my favorite local brew, and some salad makings. Then we head back to my place.

I unload the vegetables onto the kitchen counter, pull out a stool for Rachel to sit on, and pour her a glass of wine.

She's obviously not used to watching someone else cook, because she can't stand to not be helping. She keeps reaching for the knife, the measuring cup, whatever I happen to be holding. "Let me do that."

"Just sit there and look pretty," I say, and she blushes. "All those times your mom or your grandmoms cooked for me? This is nothing."

She smiles at that.

"They came for those long visits in the summer."

"Months." Her smile turns wistful. "That was after they retired. Those were my favorite times of year. But you and Connor hated it."

"Because there were three times as many adults riding our asses and catching us doing destructive shit."

She laughs. "Too true."

"But your mom always seemed happier when they were here."

She nods. "Totally. And also weirdly more frazzled."

"And someone was always cooking. I just took all that good food for granted. Do you have those recipes?" I reach for a peeler and start shaving a cucumber.

"I definitely have a few that my mom uses, and my dad's mom, but my abuelita never used recipes. She worked in a factory. So she'd get home after a long day and start rice in the rice cooker and throw together something for dinner. She still cooks that way. Meat, garlic, green pepper, onion, tomato sauce, and cumin, brown everything, cook for a while, and you've got dinner."

"Well, whatever she did, it was fucking awesome."

She gets a distant look on her face. "I see her a lot more now that I'm in Boston and only a few hours from her in New York."

Right. I'd almost let myself forget that Rachel lives three thousand miles away.

"It's been really great. I finally learned enough Spanish so the two of us can speak it together."

"I thought you took Spanish in high school?"

She nods. "Yeah, I did, but I was never fluent. My parents didn't speak it at home, and I gave my mom hell for that when I struggled with high school Spanish. They had their reasons—wanting me to 'fit in'"—she air quotes it—"and wanting to make sure my English was solid. But my mom has said a few times she'd do it differently if she had it to do over again. She's super psyched that I'm speaking it now with my grandmother—but it's funny, my mom and I still always speak English. It's like that's where my relationship with her is stored in my brain."

She reaches out a hand and tries to take a knife and a red pepper from me. "Give me that."

I shake my head. "Answer's still no."

"I can't believe you're cooking for me!"

I think that's the fifth time she's said that. It's really cute.

And also makes me mad. Because how completely fucking ridiculous is it that her ex never cooked for her? The thing about Rachel is, she's so easy to please. She's beautiful and smart and sexy and uncomplicated and the littlest things make her light up: elk jerky and cherries, the rush of jumping into the lake, learning to cast, catching her first trout, narrating a boat trip to a six-month-old, watching me cook. It doesn't take much to make her happy, and that asshole never even tried.

"What about your other grandparents?" I ask her.

"I see them, short visits, flights down to Miami, or weekends they come to see me and stay in a hotel. I miss the long visits."

I don't tell her that if she moves back to Rush Creek, she'll get the long visits back. I haven't spent much time recently at Connor's parents' house, but I know those visits still happen. But I don't want to sound like I'm trying to talk her into moving here.

I know she wouldn't.

It's not in the plan... and I would never ask her to give up the plan for me.

Rachel's manners would totally win my mom's approval. She tries to insist I should let her set the table, but I tell her I've got it. When it's time to sit, I pull out her chair for her and scooch it back in again.

She smiles up at me. "I know I'm not supposed to like that."

"Like what?" I sit across from her.

"You pulling out my chair for me. Pushing it in. I'm supposed to be strong and self-sufficient and do it for myself. But don't stop."

I laugh. "You got it."

Later tonight, I decide, I'm going to get her to say that in another context entirely. *Don't stop.*

We dig in.

"Omigod this is so good!" She's quiet for a minute. Then she says, "Can I just say, there is something about a guy who can catch and cook his own food?"

I grin. "Wait till we go camping and I catch fish in the woods with a handmade rod, roast them over an open fire, and feed you."

She puts her hand over her heart. "Shirtless?"

I chuckle. "Super impractical with the bugs and the temp, but if it works for you, sure."

"It would work for me."

"I didn't think you liked camping." I remember from high school, her turning her nose up at it when Connor and I went.

Rachel grins. "I mean, what you described is more like erotic art than camping."

I'm smiling so hard it hurts my face. I don't think that has ever happened to me. "Rachel."

"Mmm?" She has just put another giant bite of trout with black butter in her mouth, and is making a face not so different from the one she made the other day next to my motorcycle. Makes it hard to eat. Pun intended.

"I like you so damn much."

Her gaze jumps to my face, startled. And alarmed? For a second, my heart plummets.

Then she smiles, the sweetest Rachel smile I've ever seen. "I like you, too, Brody Wilder," she says. "So damn much."

"So," I say, when we've wiped out dinner. "What's for dessert?"

"Let me do the dishes first."

"Nope. I'm doing the dishes."

"You cooked! I do the dishes!"

"Nope."

I get up, cross to the sink and start washing.

She gets up, strides toward me, and tries to body check me aside. Needless to say, with probably fifty pounds of muscle on her, I don't move.

She stands behind me and sticks her arms under mine, grabbing a dish and soaping it.

"Seriously, Rachel?"

But the feel of her breasts on my back is so distracting that my protest is limp. Okay, wrong word choice. My protest is solidly upright and begging for more. I shut off the water and turn in her arms, kissing her.

It goes from zero to sixty in about three seconds. Rachel's mouth does that to me. Apparently, mine does it to her, too, because it doesn't take long before she's panting, clutching, riding my thigh. I lift her up, planning to carry her to my bedroom, but she stops me. "Wait. Let me get dessert first."

"What?"

She pulls away—not my plan—and retrieves the Rush to Read Books bag from where she left it on the counter. She opens it and removes the contents.

One small bullet vibe, one fleshlight, and a bottle of warming gel. Strawberry flavored.

"Oh, wow," I say, going from hard to harder. It's hot enough, thinking about using that vibe on her, but... "Have you been thinking about this all night?"

"Mmm-hmm," she says happily. "Where's your bedroom?"

"I'm not sure where you got your good girl reputation, but it's totally shot." I grab her hand, leading her. "Kaput. Wait. Give me a second." I make her stand in the hall while I neaten things up. Luckily it's not a total pigsty in there. My sheets are clean, there's only a few days worth of laundry tossed on the floor, and my own bottle of lube, which has been getting more than its fair share of use since Rachel came to town, is in the drawer with the box of condoms I bought yesterday.

"Okay, come in."

She does, and sets the bag on the bed.

I kiss her, stopping only long enough to strip off her shirt. I resume, managing to unbutton, unzip, and slide her pants down without interrupting the tangle of our tongues or our co-mingled groans of pleasure. Then my hand is between her legs. Her panties are damp. I reach for the Rush to Read bag, find the bullet vibe, and use my thumb to press the soft power button.

Then I hand it to her. "I want to watch."

She blushes and shakes her head. "I want you to use it on me."

"I promise. Later. Right now? I want to watch you use it."

She hesitates, then drops to the bed and brings the vibe close to the plumpest part of her mound.

With her free hand, she pushes the bag towards me. "If you get to watch me, I get to watch you."

She doesn't have to ask twice. I shed my pants like it's an Olympic sport. A moment later, I've got the fleshlight lubed up and am slowly stroking myself into it.

Not bad.

Not quite the real thing, but since Rachel has just pulled her panties off and is sliding the quietly buzzing vibe against her seam, I'm more worried about getting off too quickly.

"Look at you," I groan. Her knees have fallen apart, thighs parted, and I can see her, pink and gorgeous and glistening. "Look at you."

We're both quiet for a moment, and there's something so intense about this, about the abandoned look on her face, the motion of her hand between her legs. I can see all of her at once, and it's really, really doing it for me. I have to slow down and ease up so I can stay with her.

The vibe is right on her clit now, and her thighs are trembling. She's watching my hand. Her mouth is open, her lips soft and wet.

I have to stop stroking completely.

"Brody."

"Mmm-hmm?"

"This isn't going to make me come."

"No?"

"No." She shakes her head and glares down at it. "I'm going to need my money back. I'm going to get that Cadillac thing next time. Or maybe the rabbit?"

"Or both," I suggest. "You should probably buy stock. Would that be a conflict of interest?"

We're both laughing, and it occurs to me that I don't think I've ever thought of sex as fun before. Which probably means I was doing it wrong.

Or just with the wrong women.

She sobers up and gives me a super serious look. "Will you help me?"

My cock jerks in the clasp of silicone and my fist. "Jesus, Rachel. Of fucking course."

I reach to take the vibe from her, but she shuts it off and sets it aside, then unhooks her bra. "Your mouth."

Rachel asking for my mouth will go down for all eternity as a peak life experience.

She's so fucking pretty, leaning up on her elbows. Not just her brown-tipped tits and that small, neat strip of hair and the shine of arousal on her pussy—although hell, I'm not complaining about any of that. But the curiosity and anticipation on her face. The sexy half smile. The bright glint in her eyes.

She hands me the warming gel. "Dessert," she says, the smile getting bigger, the glint naughtier.

I kneel and tug her down to the edge of the bed. Slick her with gel. Cover her with my mouth. Even through the fake strawberry flavor, I can taste how aroused she is. Her clit is big and swollen under my tongue, probably too sensitive right now for direct contact. So I slide two fingers into her, crook them up until she gasps and lifts off the bed, and work her g-spot.

With my other hand, I reach up to play with her nipples.

Then I give her back my tongue on her clit, big, slow, circles. Not too much contact, but lots of pressure and heat.

"Oh, God, Brody," she says. "Holy fuck, that's—"

I've made her curse.

"—so good. Don't stop. Please don't stop."

And I've made her say *don't stop*.

She's lifting her hips to my mouth now, quick and eager. She's close.

I lighten up, keeping her there. Holding her at that edge for as long as I can. Until she says, "Brody, *please*."

Then I suck her clit and take her over the edge, so she's moaning my name, clenching on my fingers, and slicking my tongue.

I am never going to get enough of this. Of her.

31

He makes a small noise of satisfaction.

I can't even do that. I just lie there, limp to my toes.

Wanting him.

Even with his fingers (still) inside me, coming that hard makes me hungry for more.

"You know what I really want?"

"What do you really want, baby?" He slides his fingers out —leaving me even more empty—and swipes the back of his hand across his mouth.

"I want you inside me."

The flush on Brody's face deepens. "I want that, too."

He yanks his shirt over his head and kicks his way out of his pants and boxer briefs.

Brody Wilder stark naked is a national treasure. He's such a feast, I can't figure out where I want to look—at his golden, inked pecs, the line of dark-gold hair bisecting his eight pack, or the proud jut of his cock at the V of muscle in his hips.

What did I do to deserve this prize?

"Admiring the merch?" he teases, flexing a bit.

"Nah," I tease back, and he rolls his eyes and crawls up the bed over me, bracing himself on his arms. Which only creates an even better biceps-and-pecs scenario for ogling. Brody's built enough that he has those distinct swells of muscle—the cap of shoulder, the swell of mid-bicep, that gorgeous cut between biceps and triceps.

So. Lickable.

"Eyes up here, pretty girl," he teases, lowering himself onto me. And oh, my God, it feels good, all that warm skin against skin. I wrap my arms around him and rub myself all over him, and he groans and holds me tight, dropping kisses along my jawline until he finds my mouth. And then we're kissing so hard and so deep. Not like any other kisses we've shared. They've all been good, but this kiss says, *I need you. Now.*

And maybe forever.

I won't examine that thought right now. I won't. I clutch him closer and sink deeper into the kiss, begging him for more of his mouth, more of his hands. He is a skilled multi-tasker, kissing me and also finding my nipples with his thumb and forefinger, tweaking, rolling, pinching, flicking.

Those sensations gang up with the tension gathering in my core, and suddenly another orgasm doesn't feel far off.

Which is not my mode of operation, usually.

Brody has found my second gear, and I so appreciate it.

He rolls away from me, fumbling with the nightstand drawer, coming back with a packet in his hand. His hands are shaking. I take it from him, open it, and roll it on him.

"I want to go slow," he says.

He eases himself through the slick of arousal on my sex,

sliding back and forth over my clit. Yup, I'm going to come again, without even trying.

And as soon as I do, as soon as I buck and call his name, he plunges in and fills me, and it's so, so good. I'm coming and clenching and *needing*, and he's big and thick and hot and everything I need.

"Yeah, Rachel, just like that, you come for me, baby, you come."

He kisses me again, deep and greedy, and there's no way he's taking this slow. It feels too good—to both of us. I can't stop grabbing him and pulling him deeper. I can't stop kissing him like I want to devour him. I can't stop trying to touch him, everywhere.

His first couple of controlled, careful thrusts give way to what comes next. I feel that moment—when he realizes it. His rhythm breaks first, then the kiss. He's up, over me, eyes almost surprised, his hips jerking. Needy. Greedy. Grunts and fingers digging into my flesh.

I love it.

"That's it," I tell him. "You take what you need."

And then he doesn't even try to stay in control. He thrusts chaotically, hard, deep, rolling and grinding his hips over mine, which makes me come again. Yes. Again.

And then he's coming, mouth on mine, hands gripping me, every muscle in his body rigid.

"Rachel!"

CONDOM ATTENDED TO, he wraps me in his arms and holds me.

There are no questions about whether we'll cuddle or whether I'll stay. Who'll put on clothes or how we'll share the bed. There's just this. Brody's arms and his lips in my hair and his voice murmuring that I have just broken him because he's never had sex that good before.

Neither have I.

"Maybe it's not that you broke me," he says, a minute later. "Maybe it's that you put me back together."

I smile against his bare chest.

Another thing there is no question about:

I am in love with Brody Wilder. This is not a thing I have to agonize about, discuss with my girlfriends, or realize in a sudden, shining moment. It's just so obvious. Possibly I loved Brody Wilder from the moment he first picked me up by the side of the road where I was standing with my bike, its front tire flat.

Possibly I loved him before that, from afar, watching him play with Connor and knowing that I would always be on the outside of that boy awesomeness, telling myself I didn't care.

More likely, I fell in love with him sometime this month. Maybe when I realized that he would do just about anything to make things right for his family's business and his family. When he somehow managed to take in stride the fact that I'd unexpectedly brought sex toys on his boat. When he taught me to picnic without a plan and jump without overthinking it.

When I saw how much he loves Justin. How even through his anger and frustration, he has such a big, loving, giving heart.

It doesn't really matter. The point is, the *problem* is, I'm in love with Brody Wilder.

And I don't want to be the girl Brody Wilder fucks. I want to be the woman he loves.

I don't want to take a walk on the Wilder side.

I want to live there.

I want Brody Wilder to be the *awesome boyfriend* in step six, the man in my plan.

Now I just have to figure out how to tell him that.

32

I t takes us a long time to get out of bed the next morning. Rachel makes us coffee, and I cook us bacon and eggs.

We're not out of the bed very long, though, before we find ourselves back in it.

Not that either of us minds.

By the time we manage to get ourselves dressed and the kitchen cleaned up, it's late morning. And I still don't want Rachel to go. My eye falls on a copy of the Five Rivers Gazette that I tossed with a pile of mail on my counter. "You know what we should do? We should take Justin and go to the Five Rivers Summer Festival."

Even before the brides and grooms and spa-seekers showed up, Rush Creek was a tourist town. There's always some kind of festival going on. Quilts. Crafts. Art. Blues and Brews. Spring, summer, fall, holiday ... there's always something.

Up until now, I've never been much of a festival goer. But

if it means I get to spend another day with my two favorite people, I'm in.

Her eyes meet mine. "We might run into people we know." She's watching me carefully.

"We might." I shrug. I'm not as nonchalant as I'm pretending to be, but I'm done hiding Rachel like she's a dirty secret. I don't know what will happen next between us—there's still the huge matter of three thousand miles—but Connor definitely doesn't get to have an opinion about it.

She raises her eyebrows. "You ready for that?"

I nod. "Are you?"

She hesitates. Her gaze trails away from me, and my heart stutters over a beat. Then she looks back, brown eyes steady, and nods. "Yeah. I am."

I try to ignore the warmth that spreads in my chest. It's impossible. I quit trying. I reach for her hand and squeeze it. She squeezes back.

I've made up my mind that sometime today, maybe at the festival, I'm going to ask her if she thinks there's any future for us.

Because I do.

I don't know what it would look like. It might be hard. It might mean long distance or sacrifice on one of our parts—but I have to at least ask.

For now, though, I content myself with bending down to kiss her.

And of course, we have to make one more trip back to bed before we finally make it out the door.

WE GRAB Justin from Zoë's—no muss, no fuss—and head to the festival. Rush Creek is just one of the sites for the summer fair, but there's still a lot going on. We throw a blanket down in the shade near one of the music stages and let Justin kick his pudgy bare feet while we listen to Logjam, a rock band started by a couple of Connor's and my friends. After a while that gives way to some seriously lame singer-songwriter on solo guitar, and Rachel and I exchange a look. We don't even have to say it out loud. We just pack up, strap Justin back into the Baby Bjorn carrier, facing out, and wander off to explore the food booths.

We probably should get real food, but neither of us wants to, so we buy elephant ears and garlic fries. Rachel offers Justin small bites of her food, which Zoë said would be okay as long as I didn't give him anything he could choke on. He gums them with gusto, whapping his hands and shouting his approval, then drools most of the contents of his mouth into the space between his chest and the carrier. That'll be fun later.

We end up in the kids' section of the festival. Justin seems uninterested in the juggler and I don't think he'll get anything out of the face painting. It'll just end up all over me and Rachel.

And then we strike the motherlode of kid joy.

Touch a Truck day.

"Justin, look!" I tell him as we step around the high school. Justin is still in the Baby Bjorn, strapped to my chest and facing out. I'm holding Rachel's hand. Which feels amazing. I'm slowly realizing I don't think I've held anyone else's hand before Rachel's.

It's so fucking nice.

"That's a school bus, Jus. When you get bigger, you'll go to school like the big kids, and that's how you'll get there," Rachel tells him.

I'm sure he has no idea what she's saying, but he bounces with excitement anyway. And maybe it's just the little kid in me, but I don't see how anyone couldn't think this was awesome. Fire trucks, police cruisers, backhoes, school buses —plus loads and loads of other kids, running around and providing extra visual entertainment.

And apparently Justin is a huge fan, because he goes from bouncing to kicking and—

I double over, clutching my junk and groaning.

"Brody?"

Rachel is leaning over us, understandably concerned.

"Gah——d—daaang—it. He kicked me in the balls."

She's trying not to laugh, and I'm trying not to die.

"Fu—g. Fuh, gah."

Now she's definitely laughing. "*Son of a biscuit* always works for me in a pinch," she offers.

I glare at her, and she makes a contrite face.

I turn my glare on Justin, who is all big-eyed innocence. "He got bigger since the last time I had him in this thing." I slowly straighten up, still trying to tamp down that bone-deep sick feeling that comes with taking a shot to the jewels.

"You okay?" she asks.

"I will be. In a year or so."

"Want me to take him?" She holds out her arms.

I unfasten one side of the Bjorn and pass Justin to Rachel.

"Do you want the carrier?"

Working the carrier requires some serious advanced skill, and it takes both Rachel and me using all the contents of our big noggins several minutes to get the carrier on her chest and Justin in the carrier.

"Did you do that on purpose?" she asks when I brush my fingers over her nipple, which is taut and peaked under her tight-fitting t-shirt.

"I may have." I grin lazily at her, then lean down and kiss her over Justin's head. He is still kicking madly, so I keep one hand loosely cupped near my crotch, just in case I want to give him fun cousins one day.

She reaches into her pocket and pulls out her phone, her eyes roaming over the screen. She smiles, then bites her lip.

"What is it?"

"My mom got a clean bill of health at the doctor's. She's off crutches."

"Oh, that's great!" I say reflexively, before I realize: It's not so great. It means Rachel can go back to Boston.

Not that I thought the moment could be postponed indefinitely. I always knew it was coming. Rachel is a woman with a plan, and I'm her vacation from reality.

"So you can book tickets home now," I say. "You must be psyched to get the plan back on track."

"Uh," she says. "Yeah."

"So you go back, you move in with, what's your friend's name? Louisa? You go back to your library job? And then, onwards to the awesome boyfriend, right?"

Please, I think. *Please don't.*

"Brody," she repeats.

But just then, a familiar voice says, "Well, well, well," and I look up to find a gaggle of Wilders and assorted relatives. Gabe, Easton, Lucy, Hanna, Amanda, Heath, the kids, and my mom.

The voice in question, of course, belongs to Amanda.

Rachel blushes wildly. Justin kicks, elated to be surrounded by a pack of his favorite people.

"Look at this picture of domestic bliss," Amanda teases me. I'm not sure if I want to punch her or hug her.

We exchange a round of warm Wilder greetings and hugs.

Rachel works open the carrier so she can pass Justin around, and various Wilders take him, one by one, and coo in his face.

The world must seem like a really fucking weird place to babies.

But I've got bigger worries on my mind. Because hustling up behind my family, hands full of cotton candy, is Connor.

He looks from me to Rachel and back again.

"What the—?"

"Connor," Rachel and I say, at exactly the same time.

He puts up both hands. "Don't. Just—save it, okay?" He gives me a look made of laser beams and loathing. "You *asshole*." It's soft and dangerous. His hands are clenched into fists, and for a second, I think he's going to bury one in my face, phalanx of Wilder backup be damned.

But he doesn't.

He shoves the cotton candy bouquet into Amanda's hands, turns, and stalks off.

I shoot an agonized look at Rachel.

"Go," she says. "I've got Justin."

I go.

"Connor."

He ignores me.

"Connor!"

He breaks into a run.

I chase him all the way to the parking lot and manage to grab his arm right before he reaches his truck. "Connor. It's not what you think."

"What do I think?" he demands. "You tell me what I think. You fucking explain to me what I think."

I take a step back, let his arm drop. "She and I—we—"

He raises both eyebrows. "Oh, Jesus, Brody, what kind of fucking mess have you made?"

It's a blade between the ribs.

We're both out of breath from the run, and he's glaring at me so fiercely that it hurts. In all the years I've known Connor, he's never gotten mad at me like this.

He really, really fucking doesn't want me with his sister.

I need to not think about that too hard.

"This isn't just me getting my rocks off, Con. I care about her. A lot."

"Jesus, Brody." Connor's head is down, but when it comes up, I see something in his eyes that shakes me to the core. Pity. "Dude. This is what I was fucking afraid of. *This* is why I told you to leave her alone. I knew one of you was going to wreck the other one and I'd have to pick up the pieces."

"What are you talking about?" I demand.

"I'm talking about the fact that you are obviously in so deep here, and she's just—"

He winces.

"What?"

"I heard her say something to her friend. On the phone. I didn't put it together, because I didn't know then that you were—" He hesitates again. "—*with* my sister. But now I know she was talking about you. And it was a while back, so maybe it doesn't mean anything. But I just thought you should know. Maybe it'll make it easier to walk away."

I'm staring at him with a sensation in my gut like wet concrete. "She said it was her"—his hands come up in air quotes—"walk on the Wilder side."

Walk on the Wilder side.

"She didn't mean it that way," I say.

"Maybe not," Connor says. But he doesn't sound convinced.

"When was that?"

"It was a while ago," he admits. "Couple of weeks at least."

"Things were different then."

"Different how?" he asks.

"We hadn't—we weren't—"

But when I think about it, when I go to explain to him

what's happened, it melts away like sugar in water, insubstantial. We have spent lots of time together, but never, in all that time, did she suggest that she might want to drop the plan. She never said I was more to her than a good time or that she was weighing the possibility of putting Boston on hold.

So maybe it's not so different now.

"I'm going to talk to her," I say, trying to hold onto the confidence that I felt earlier today, when we put Justin in the carrier on her chest. Or the confidence I felt yesterday when I made her come with my mouth. "I'm going to ask her to stay."

"Brody, *no*," Connor says, sounding so alarmed that my heart grinds to a stop. He's shaking his head. "Please don't."

I don't think I've ever seen him this serious about anything. Not even the time he begged me not to ask Julia Shree to the senior prom because he was—he claimed at the time—in love with her.

I didn't.

He wasn't.

But the point is, Connor is pleading with me.

"Please don't, Brody. She's been through way more than enough. I'm asking you not to make this complicated for her. Just, put a nice neat ending on it. Closure. Tell her you had a really good time but you know she's got a life in Boston. You've known Rachel her whole life, Brody. She wants it all. The white wedding dress and the suburban house and the Ivy League husband. She needs things nice and organized and steady. Predictable. She needs to keep things neat. Let her go back there and live in her sublet with her friend Louisa and take her librarian job. Let her meet a guy who'll take good care of her and make it easy for her."

A guy who'll take good care of her and make it easy for her.

I can almost see it. The kind of guy Connor means. They meet at a party with some friends. Or maybe an event connected to the library. A library fundraiser. He's there in dress pants and a button-down shirt, and he chats with her about books they've both read. He asks her out to a nice restaurant and drives her around in his Prius, and he lets dates three, four, and five pass without putting the moves on her because he wants to make sure they're really comfortable with each other first.

"And you're—" Connor rakes a hand through his hair. "You're not—"

He stops.

"I'm not that guy," I say, so he doesn't have to.

He scowls. "Jesus, Brody, I didn't say that."

"You didn't have to."

This is Connor. My best friend. The guy who has been with me through thick and thin. The guy who knows—who should know—that I would never do anything to hurt his sister. Who should see that I am fiercely loyal and totally faithful and trying so fucking hard to turn this ship around and make myself into the kind of man who deserves a woman like Rachel.

And if he can't see it?

Maybe it's not there.

Maybe all the people who didn't think I had it in me to take care of the people they loved—my dad, Gabe, Zoë...

Maybe they were onto something.

I travel with the pack of Wilders, waiting for Brody to come back. I've got Justin back in the Björn, and he's dozing with his little cheek pressed against my chest. He's warm and heavy and I think I'll implode from the cuteness.

Finally Brody comes back, alone, with his head down. Damn, that can't be good. The Wilders apparently think we need space, because they immediately drift away, citing all the other places they need to be—main stage, food booths, home.

"Hey," I say to Brody, when they're gone. "Everything okay? Ish?"

He shrugs. "I mean, yes and no. He didn't punch me in the face and I don't think he's going to kill me."

I smile at that. "I'm grateful for that. I'd miss you if he did."

His head swings up, just enough for me to catch a flash of green. "Will you miss me? When you go?"

This is it: This is the moment to ask him how he'd feel if I said I was thinking about staying. For *him*.

"Will you miss your walk on the Wilder side?"

He says it almost like a tease, but the familiar words catch me with a jolt, and I can hear the hurt. Plus his head's still down. No eye contact.

"Did Connor—?"

He nods.

"Brody. I'm sorry. I'm so sorry. I should never have said that Wilder thing, even as a joke. It was more about me than about you."

"I know," he says. "You had to prove something about yourself. That you weren't any kind of girl. And you did."

"No—I mean, that wasn't all it was, Brody. It might have started that way, but it became something else."

He lifts his head, turns toward me. And stares at me. Green eyes, long lashes, his hair rumpled. His stubble is golden.

He has never looked more beautiful to me, and I know that the more I get to know Brody Wilder, the more beautiful he will be.

And I can't read his expression at all.

"I care about you, Brody. A lot."

Say it, Rachel. Say you've fallen in love with him. Tell him you love him.

I almost say it: I love you, Brody. I want to stay, if you want me to.

But I don't get the words out before he says, "It's been a good adventure, Rach. And I'll be sorry when it's over."

Wait.

This isn't how it's supposed to go.

This isn't the plan.

The thought stops my breathing.

Have I done it again, without even meaning to? Have I leapt so far ahead in my fantasy world that I stopped clearly seeing the man right in front of me? Have I written a whole plan for a man who wants nothing to do with it?

As if he can hear the voice in my head, he says, "You can pick up your plan right where you left off. Like you said, you didn't even lose too much ground. You have your job again, in Boston, the apartment with Louisa."

Now, Rachel. *Now.*

"But *you're* here."

"Rachel," he says, sounding tired. Like it hurts him to say my name. "I'm not the guy in the plan. I don't—"

We lock eyes. Something stills in his, like a spark that has flickered and gone dark.

"You don't what, Brody?"

He shakes his head. "I'm really fucking sick of not being the man people need me to be, Rachel. I couldn't do that to you. You'd end up resenting me."

"That's not true, Brody!" Can I make him believe me? "You've never disappointed me, and I know you won't start now."

But he won't look at me. I can't even see his eyes; they're hidden by the fall of his hair.

And all of a sudden I get it.

"You don't *want* to be the guy in the plan," I say dully.

I wait for him to fight me.

I wait for him to *look* at me.

But without lifting his head, he shakes it, and I know it's over.

How ironic, I think. Werner wanted me to the be the girl he married, but not the girl he fucked. And Brody wants the opposite.

"Okay," I say. "Okay."

He holds out his arms. For a brief, startlingly wonderful moment, I think he is holding out his arms for me. I think we are going to be okay, that I misunderstood him.

But as I start to step forward, I remember the weight on my chest. Justin.

He's holding out his arms to take Justin.

He waits patiently while I unstrap the carrier. My hands are shaking, and I think he sees that, but he doesn't reach out to help. I'm glad he doesn't; I don't know what I'd do if he touched me now.

Probably start to cry.

To distract myself, I kiss Justin on the top of his head. When I lift my face, Brody looks away.

"So that's—it," I say.

He nods, without looking at me. And then he turns away, completely, opens the truck door, and settles Justin into his car seat.

I stand there, helpless, watching, wanting to say something, anything, the one right thing that will change the outcome.

Even though I know that thing doesn't exist.

I take a deep breath.

I walk away.

Just about the time I get to the edge of the parking lot, the engine roars to life. And then he pulls out of the parking lot and he's gone.

I double over, out of breath and out of shape and hurting so bad in my stomach and chest that I'm not sure I'll ever be able to draw a full breath again.

RACHEL

I'd forgotten that Brody and I have to do one more party together on the boat. It's a group of college students this time, friends from the University of Washington— a totally different vibe from the partiers so far. Most of the students are much savvier about toys, having grown up on a steady diet of Internet ads, Tumbler gifs, and Rule 34.

Rule 34, I learn, states that *If something exists, there is porn of it. No exceptions.*

"The rule came about when a comic artist on the web learned that there was Calvin and Hobbes porn," their de facto ringleader tells me.

"Oh, *God!*" I say miserably.

I want to look at Brody, to see if this makes him as unhappy as it makes me, but it hurts too much to look at Brody. Blank-faced, stoic Brody. Not even a scowl to let me know he's in there. And the few times I've tried to catch his eye, he's turned away. Not that he's ignoring me. He was entirely civil to me as we loaded the boat. He held out his arm so I could balance myself climbing in. He has been nothing but polite.

And I hate it.

My chest has not stopped aching since he told me that he doesn't want to be the guy in my plan. Not that I should have been surprised. If you decide to bag the bad boy, it's pure fantasy to think that you'll live happily ever after with him. Especially if the two of you reside on opposite sides of the country and are as different as two people can be.

Still, knowing that doesn't stop the pain.

"Rachel?" Ringleader asks me.

I get back to business.

In addition to the savvy students, there are also a few in the group who are like me: they grew up knowing this stuff was around but never quite got up the courage to delve into it. Maybe they were afraid their browsing histories would keep them out of college, maybe they were afraid to own toys in a household with nosy little siblings, or maybe they just kept meaning to get around to it and never found time.

So I aim my chatter at them, and like almost everyone who's brave enough to attend a party in the first place, they eventually open up, asking questions, and, well, buying a truckload of new toys.

I'm going to miss this, too. Part of me thinks maybe I'll get my own Real Romance business when I get back to Boston, but I'm not sure how that'll work with a full-time job. And maybe it's just a fantasy, too, that I'll be able to capture and keep part of Rush Creek Rachel when I go home.

Maybe Rush Creek Rachel only existed for a brief, glorious moment.

Maybe I need to let her go, too.

I FLY HOME TO BOSTON. Louisa picks me up at the airport and brings me to the large apartment she shares with her two friends. I really like both of them. They're fun, lively, and kind. And my room passes muster. It's bigger than I was expecting—probably a good fifteen-by-fifteen—and gets western light through two big windows. We all use the same kitchen, but everyone is generous about sharing and great about respecting each other's stuff, and it even looks like we might set up a rotation so we can each cook one or two dinners a week.

I go back to work for the library, this time for a librarian named Brenna Cho, who is also a great boss. I learn the ins and outs of the adult desk, memorize answers to the most common questions our patrons ask, and generally start thinking like an adult librarian. I make myself indispensable there. Brenna says the day Hettie let me go was the best day of her working life, and I know she means it. It turns out I like working with adult readers just as much as I liked working with kids, which surprises me. Maybe it's because adults are basically just big kids, especially when you get them excited about a new book. Maybe a little slower moving but more likely to wash their hands in the bathroom.

Or not.

In the evenings, I sit in the shared living room. My mom and I finished watching *Crash Landing on You* before I left Rush Creek, so now I've moved on to *Start-Up*. I binge watch episodes and ugly cry when things go wrong for Dal Mi. When it gets too late to start a new episode, I don't want to go to bed, so I stay on the couch flipping through my Instagram feed.

Brody doesn't have an Insta, but Amanda, Lucy, and Wilder Adventures all do. So does my mom's Real Romance business, and that's how I find out she's still doing the parties on the boat. She reposts a photo from Wilder, too, so I hop over there, and see that Brody's new concept is going great guns. There are photos of Jem leading a book club, of Nan's gorgeous baked goods (also reposted on the Rush Creek Bakery feed), and of the Glory Day Spa massage sessions, complete with blissed out customers.

In the background of one of the photos, I can just make out Brody, and I enlarge the photo to see the expression on his face.

Louisa snatches the phone out of my hands.

"What the—?"

"You've been on that couch for three hours and twenty-three minutes," she accuses. "And last night you were on it for four hours and twelve minutes."

"Louisa!"

"I timed you," she says, frowning at me.

"I'm tired," I protest.

"You're not *tired*," she says. "You're marinating in your own misery. Get off that couch and come out with me."

"Where—?"

"Brusque." She's not accusing me of being short with her; that's the name of a new bar in Davis Square that she's been trying to convince me to try with her for almost a week. Apparently, a new young singles pickup scene is coalescing there.

Nothing in the phrase "young singles pickup scene"

appeals to me in the slightest, but there's no arguing with Louisa, so I drag myself off the couch and head to my room to try to find something decent to wear.

I stand in front of my closet and stare at the possibilities.

Or lack of possibilities, maybe.

That's where she finds me, fifteen minutes later. I haven't moved.

"Rachel," she says quietly. "I'm really, really worried about you."

"Don't worry," I say, reflexively. Then I hear myself and sigh. "I'm really not miserable. This is a great setup for me." I indicate the room. "It's a great room. This is a great house. I have a great job. Objectively speaking, everything's perfect."

Louisa crosses her arms. She looks extra scary. "Rachel. Do you hear yourself?"

"Wha—?" I start to ask, but all of a sudden, I do.

Perfect.

Perfect job, perfect apartment, perfect setup, perfect situation.

It's all exactly right, except it's really, truly, all just wrong.

Two weeks after the summer festival, Connor finds me washing the boat outside Gabe's and Wilder. I don't set down the sponge or look at him, but I can feel him standing just off my shoulder, breathing.

He should be uneasy, because even if he was right, he was a dick about it.

"Hey," he says. "I, um, thought you might want to know. Rachel went back to Boston."

"Thanks."

I still don't look at him.

"Hey," he says again. "I heard you got kicked out of Oscar's last night."

I close my eyes. Fucking small towns. "I didn't get kicked out. I just got cut off."

And the night before that, too, but who's counting.

"Jill said you seem pretty miserable."

I don't bother to answer that. If your own best friend has to hear from someone else that you're miserable, you shouldn't have to explain it to him.

"I'm, um, really..." He takes a deep breath. Connor's not exactly a big talker, either, so I know this isn't easy for him, but there is no fucking way in hell I'm letting him off the hook. Let him stew in his own juices. "I'm really sorry."

Now I turn around. In almost thirty years of friendship, I have never heard Connor apologize for anything.

"For fucking things up between you guys."

"Isn't that what you were trying to do?" I ask him.

He shifts uneasily, not meeting my eyes. "What do you mean by that?"

"Just what I said."

And to his credit, he doesn't deny it. He just says, "Yeah. I guess. I mean, it just seemed like such a bad idea. And if it went south, I didn't want to have to pick up the pieces on either side. But if I'd known how much you liked her—"

I shrug, because it hurts less that way.

"It's fine, Connor. It wasn't going to happen. She has a plan, and it doesn't call for being with a guy who can't pull it together in any aspect of his life."

I turn back to the boat, working over an algae stain.

Behind me, he takes a deep breath.

"So my mom was right."

"About what?"

"She said I needed to apologize to you. And not just for fucking things up between you and Rachel. She said I needed to say I was sorry for hurting you." He clears his throat. "Did I... hurt you?"

The way he asks this actually manages to make me laugh. Connor's no dummy, but we're not guys who talk about our emotions a ton. Or ever. And he makes it sound like it's the craziest thing he's ever heard, that I might have feelings and he might have hurt them. Like it's dirty, too, the way some of the women sound when they first start talking about sex on the boat. Like the words feel foreign and awkward and wrong.

"Yeah, I mean, I figured that was bullshit," Connor says, laughing, too, relieved.

"No," I say.

I'm not sure where it comes from. It would be so much easier to let this drop. But I can't.

"No, she's right. You did hurt me."

I turn around and face him.

"You've been my best friend since forever, Con, and you all but told me I don't rate your sister. That's fucked up."

He looks like I've struck him. "Jesus, Bro."

I'm quiet, letting him think about it, and after a moment he says, "Is that what I said?"

"Not in those words, but yeah."

He nods. "Brody. I'm so fucking sorry."

This is why my mother believes in the power of a heartfelt apology. I'm not going to say my heart grows two sizes in that minute or that I instantly stop being hurt or pissed or sad. But my skin does feel less too-tight, my heart less bruised.

Connor groans. "Don't make me do this, Brody."

"Do what?" I'm genuinely curious, because he looks like he's in serious physical pain right now.

"Don't make me say—" He rubs both his hands over his face. "I mean, Jesus, okay? I was jealous. You guys hanging out all that time, having a blast, and neither of you saying anything to me. Leaving me out of it completely. I'm not super-human, Brody. She's my sister and you're my best friend."

His eyes meet mine for the first time in this whole conversation.

A lot of stuff suddenly makes sense.

Connor was a dick because he was jealous.

He said a lot of shit he probably meant *at the time*.

Some of it probably was true.

Some of it probably was not.

I hear my own voice, saying back to him, *I'm not that guy*.

What would Rachel say to that?

I know exactly what she'd have said, if I'd given her the chance:

You're not any kind of guy. You're just Brody.

And here's the thing. If I'd let her say it to me?

I might even have believed it.

Connor and I talk a while longer. Not about anything much. Just the kind of talk you do when you're trying to make things normal again after they've gotten all fucked up. It works, most of the way. I feel like we'll be okay someday. Probably.

After Connor leaves, I knock at the house.

Gabe comes out. He looks me over. "You look like shit."

"It's been a long week. Can I come in?"

He nods.

"There's something I have to tell you."

Gabe cocks his head. "Should I sit down?"

"I don't know. Maybe."

He goes into the other room and comes back with a bottle of Jameson. He takes a swig from the bottle, then hands it to me. I drink and hand it back to him.

He gestures to the couch and we both sit. Lucy's nowhere in sight; I'm guessing she's at work still.

"So what's this thing you have to tell me?" Gabe asks.

"It's about Justin and Zoë."

He gives me a long level look. "Are you going to tell me he's not yours? Because I already know."

"How—!"

"Amanda told us. She heard it from a friend."

"Us? Easton? Clark? Kane?"

He nods, mouth tight.

"Mom?"

"Yeah."

"When?" I demand.

"Three months ago?" he hazards. "It was right after Lucy came back. But no one wanted to make you talk about it."

All this time, I haven't been protecting them. They've been protecting me.

Something that has been knotted up tight in my chest unwinds just a tiny bit.

"If I had known any sooner," Gabe says, jaw tight, "I would have killed Len Dix myself that night in Oscar's."

"The truth is," I tell him, "it's as much Zoë's fault as his, if not more. And I can't kill her. Justin loves her too much. So I just have to fucking suck it up."

"I'm sorry," he says. "I know how much you love that kid."

"Rachel says—" I grimace, but it needs to be said, and she was the one who said it. "Rachel says I shouldn't let the fact that he's not mine keep me from having a relationship with him."

"Rachel's wise. How's she doing?"

"I don't know," I confess.

"You haven't reached out to her at all?"

I shake my head.

"Because of Connor?"

"Because of... me."

"You, um, want to tell me what happened?"

I do. Gabe listens, and to his ever-loving credit, says absolutely nothing until I'm done. Then he says, "A walk on the Wilder side, huh?" He's smirking. "Can't believe I never thought of that one."

I wince.

"I mean, there are worse things she could say about you."

"It just hurt. I get so tired of being the resident bad boy," I say. "Women who want to lick my tattoos and ride on my bike and get fucked against a brick wall."

"Doesn't sound all that bad to me," Gabe says wryly.

"Easy for you to say. You're the guy everyone wants. The one who's stalwart in a crisis. The family man. The son a man asks to take care of the business and his family."

As soon as the words are out of my mouth, I want to take them back. Because Gabe's no dummy.

He crosses his arms. "This is about Dad."

I shake my head, but I'm not fooling anyone.

"Jesus, Brody. I had no idea. Why didn't you ever say anything?"

"What was I going to say? Daddy didn't leave me in charge! Waaah! Waaah! Of course he didn't fucking leave me in charge. I was a screwup."

"No." There's something in Gabe's expression. A kind of wonder. "You were a fourteen-year-old boy. And it didn't even fucking cross my mind that you'd feel like you'd been shut out." His eyes rake over my face, and it occurs to me that one of the things I hate most about Gabe is that he can see right through me.

I reach for the whiskey and he hands it over. I don't slug it, though. I just hold the bottle. It's helpful to have something to grip.

I take a deep breath. "I was only a year younger than you."

He nods.

"But Dad never said anything to me about helping out or taking care of anyone. I could see you struggling after he died and when Mom was sick but when I asked if I could help, you said I'd screw it up."

"I was fifteen," Gabe says. He doesn't sound defensive. He just sounds *thoughtful*. Like he's also sorting this out, finally. "And I was terrified, too. Dad left me in charge. I felt like he was watching to make sure I didn't fuck up."

I'm sure my mouth is open.

For the first time ever, I think, *I got it all wrong*. Gabe didn't get the prize. He got left holding the bag.

It makes it easier to tell him the rest. "When you thought you were going to New York to be with Lucy, you left the business to Clark."

Gabe looks surprised, but then he nods. "I thought you had too much on your plate. With Justin and Zoë. I didn't want to pile any more shit on you. And let's face it, Brody, you weren't in a great place. You weren't exactly screaming 'management material.' But I get it. You'd just gotten slammed with about the worst news a guy can hear. I just wish you'd told me. I could have helped."

I take a minute, because if I talk now, I can tell my voice is going to crack, and I'm enough of a boneheaded Wilder not to want to show my big brother that weakness.

"I wish I'd told you, too."

My voice cracks anyway. And the world doesn't end.

He gives me a minute, not saying anything.

"Gabe."

"Yeah?"

"I want to help with the business, but it feels like you'd rather work yourself to the bone than ask me."

He frowns, and for a second I think he's going to argue with me, but he nods. "And that's on me, not you. I'm learning. I'm figuring it out. When Lucy went back to New York, before I realized I wanted to go after her, Mom said something to me that made a fuckton of sense. She said even though Dad laid all this responsibility on me, what he really wanted most for me was to be happy. And that that meant asking for help when I needed it. But as you can see, I still fucking suck at it."

He narrows his eyes at me. "You know what I think?"

"You're going to tell me no matter what, right?"

I'm pretty sure he's trying to hide a smile. He says, "If Connor doesn't believe you deserve Rachel, so fucking what? I'd wager Rachel doesn't give a shit. But I don't think this was ever about whether Connor thought you deserved her. It was about whether you did."

Staggered, I stare at him.

He returns my stare, unblinking.

Is that true?

I think about it.

About how I was the one who finished Connor's sentence. About how I was the one who prodded Rachel to say I didn't want to be the guy in the plan.

All this time, I was waiting for someone to choose me, to tell me I was the guy they could trust with what mattered most to them.

And it turns out this whole time? I was the one who

needed to choose myself.

I was the one who needed to figure out what needed to be done...

And fucking do it.

"Gabe."

This time, my voice doesn't crack at all. It's perfectly steady.

"Yeah?"

"I think Wilder needs a business development lead. And I think I should be it."

It takes Gabe a long time—we eldest Wilders are slow to warm up—but eventually I get his smile.

Louisa sits on the side of the bed and watches me fold the last scarf onto the top of my suitcase.

"I'm going to miss you so much," she says. "But I am so proud of you."

"I'm terrified," I admit to her.

"I know, kiddo." She sighs. "So much bigger than pulling a scarf out of a drawer without looking."

I'm going back to Rush Creek. And I don't have a plan. Not even a little one.

All I have is the knowledge that Rush Creek Rachel is who I want to be, the certainty that I belong close to my family, and the strong suspicion that I gave up too easily on Brody. Not much to build a cross-country move on...

Which I guess is the whole point. Not having a plan means trusting those things: Your vision for yourself, your sense of what's true—instead of a perfect-on-paper to-do list.

Also, let's be totally honest: It's not exactly flying without a net if you know you can crash in your childhood bedroom.

But I gotta start somewhere.

I zip up my bags, which Louisa helps me carry down to the front door.

She opens her arms and I hug the heck out of her. I make her promise to come visit me in Rush Creek as soon as she can, and she makes me promise not to be a stranger to Boston. She lets me go, and I bend down to pick up my suitcases.

There's a knock at the door.

Louisa gets up on tiptoes—she's teeny—and then turns to look at me with huge eyes.

"There's a very beautiful man standing on the porch," she whispers. "He has bed hair and two days worth of scruff and green eyes and lots of tattoos."

And then she grabs my arm and lets out a long, silent squeal, and runs away to leave me facing the door.

I open it.

"Hey," Brody says.

Oh, my God, he looks good. Tired, yes, and Louisa wasn't kidding about the scruff, but that's definitely a feature, not a bug. He's got his arms crossed and his eyes down and that bad-boy off-center back-on-his-heels thing going, and my whole body pretty much tunes into his station.

I try to say *hey* back, but my voice fails me. I try again. "Hey."

"I want to be part of the plan," he says.

It's slowly dawning on me that Brody Wilder has just flown across the entire country to tell me he wants to be with me. My heart is pounding, my pulse beating in my throat. My hands are icy.

"I've spent my whole fucking life feeling like I wasn't invited to the party, when the truth is that I was too busy blowing off the party so I wouldn't feel shitty if I didn't get an invitation."

"Oh," I say, because this makes perfect sense. In fact, it makes everything about Brody make sense.

"I did it with Justin, with Gabe, with you—and I'm not fucking doing it anymore. There are things I want, Rachel. I want Justin in my life. I want to be Gabe's partner—like, for real. And—"

Brody is looking at me with the full, unfiltered force of those green eyes, and they are wrecking me. Or maybe it's the longing and the hunger in them.

"I want you. And I have a plan. For the first time in my entire life, I have a plan."

I start laughing.

"Jesus, Rachel," he says, taken aback. "That wasn't exactly the response I was expecting."

I stop laughing immediately, but of course I have to explain. I step back, opening the door wider so he can see my two suitcases, sitting there.

"I was coming back to Rush Creek. Without a plan."

"Oh," he says. Just that. And then his arms are around me and his mouth is on mine, and it's—

Well, honestly, it's perfect. The real, messy, complicated, imperfect kind of perfect.

It takes a humongous effort of will to stop kissing him long enough to say, "I just booked an Uber to the airport. Give me thirty seconds to cancel that and my flight."

I have barely hung up the phone when he starts kissing me again, and I lead him down the hall to my bedroom, in which, sadly, the bed is unmade because my sheets are packed in my suitcase. But maybe that's for the best because it turns out that standing-up sex is a perfectly good way to show someone how much you missed them and how much you want them to be part of your plan, or not-plan, as the case may be.

☙

AFTERWARDS, once we get our clothes all restored to their rightful places and the condom disposed of, Brody describes how things went without me. First, he tells me about his conversation with Connor, then about his conversation with Gabe.

"I love that you gave yourself a promotion."

"Yeah," he says, pleased. "I guess I did."

I frown. "I still need to have a talk with Connor. I'm still really pissed that he went off on you like that. Like I needed protection from you or something. It's insulting to both of us."

Brody strokes my cheek. "Don't be too hard on him. He told me he was jealous, which I don't think was easy for him to say."

"I'll only yell at him a little bit."

He grins.

"So, after you talked to Gabe, you bought a plane ticket and flew out here?"

He gets a slightly sheepish look his face. "Well, yes, and no. I bought a plane ticket. But it was two days out, because holy shit summer flights fill up fast. I had some time to kill. So I called a lawyer."

"You—what?"

"I called a lawyer. About Justin. And custody."

I guess I give him a dirty look, because he hastily says, "I'm not using the lawyer against Zoë. It was her idea, actually. We talked about Justin, and—here's the thing. He's not mine genetically, but the birth certificate does have my name on it. Because... well, Zoë technically committed fraud. Theoretically, I should have my name taken off and Len's put on, but when I suggested that to Zoë, just to, you know, straighten everything out so it's legal, it started us both thinking. So she reached out to Len. And he's willing to waive paternity."

"Oh. Wow."

"Yeah. What the lawyer said is that if Len waives rights, the court might very well be willing to grant them to me, because they tend to be sympathetic in cases where the petitioner has lived with the mother and child for a period of time."

"Which you did, with Zoë and Justin."

"Exactly," he says. "If Len waives his rights and I ask for them..."

"You have a really good chance of getting them."

"That's right. And Zoë is open to it, even though theoretically I could use my new powers to try to get fifty-fifty custody—"

"But you won't."

"But I won't. And she gets something out of it, because I'll have to pay child support. Which, God, Rachel, I'd do in a heartbeat."

"I know you would," I say, and lean my head on his shoulder. "Brody, that's so, so good. I'm so happy for you."

"I wanted to be able to come here and tell you I'd move to Boston for you," he says quietly, stroking my hair. "Like Gabe did for Lucy. Give up everything, move to the East Coast. And if that's what it took, I would, I swear, but because of Justin, I felt like I had to ask you if you'd move to Rush Creek."

"Apparently you didn't have to ask me," I say.

And tell him my story. About how nothing felt good or right (let alone perfect) in the weeks since I'd been back. About how much I missed Rush Creek, Amanda, Lucy, Hanna, Connor, my parents—Brody's brothers, even. About how much I missed the groups of women on the boat, and their unexpected frankness, the way something that was silly and fun and sexy could unlock changes in lives.

"And I felt like you and I weren't done," I say.

"We're not." Brody ducks his head and kisses me. "We're definitely not done. We're just getting started."

That makes me smile.

"So I decided I would just walk up to the edge and jump. See what happened."

"And this happened."

"Yeah," I say happily. "This happened."

The sweet spot between a plan and no plan is what Rachel and I do next.

First, we help her abuelita, Caridad, pack up her Washington Heights apartment, get her belongings loaded on a moving truck, and drive her to the airport. Rachel's mom will meet her on the other end.

While we're doing that, Caridad plies us with endless Cuban cooking. She speaks to Rachel mostly in Spanish. Sometimes Rachel sends me apology eyes since I understand about twenty percent of what they're saying, but the thing is, I kind of love it. I especially love it in the evening when they watch telenovelas together and talk back to the characters while I tie flies at the coffee table. From time to time, I catch myself just watching Rachel smiling and laughing.

Once Caridad's things are packed and we get her on a plane, Rachel and I rent an RV and drive back across the country.

First, of course, I recruit Kane to run Brody's Boat for a couple of weeks. I promise him I'll make it up to him by helping him plan the winter festival, Tinsel and Tatas Gala & Games, this winter.

I check in with Gabe to make sure he can do without me for those two weeks. He tells me to check in occasionally and to keep an eye out for some trip ideas to assuage Lucy's unending hunger for new concepts. (I'm getting the feeling Gabe's sexual fortunes rise and fall depending on whether he can satisfy that hunger of Lucy's. Though I don't think he minds, as long as he's satisfying Lucy somehow or other.)

I let Zoë know the travel situation, too, because I know she's been hoping for some Justin coverage. Both my mother and Amanda have been talking about nothing other than the fact that Justin has started turning his head when you say his name, so I don't think Zoë will have any trouble getting the childcare she needs.

All this checking in with people and making sure I'm exactly where I need to be feels extremely weird and foreign.

And really fucking good.

Meanwhile, Rachel has absolutely zero responsibilities, which she says feels really "dang good."

We decide to follow the Oregon Trail, of course, mostly because I want to show Rachel Yellowstone, which she's never seen, and because the best fly fishing is along that route. And yes, I have my gear with me. I don't leave home without it, because you never know when you might stumble on a quiet river.

We spot many of them, and Rachel looks beautiful in all of them, sun glinting off the hidden highlights in her dark hair and turning her skin an even deeper tan.

Her casting is getting really good, and one night, she makes me teach her how to tie a simple fly. We sit for a long time with all my materials spread out. Her fingers are smaller than mine, and even though she has less experience, she gets good at it quickly.

She says she understands why I like it so much, why I think it's such good meditation.

We never know where we're going to stop or stay until we get there, which scares the shit out of Rachel. And also, she loves it.

We sleep out under the stars most of the time. The RV mostly gets used at night for the pre-sleep activities we engage in, frequently and vigorously.

Our last stop is Tierney Bay on the Oregon Coast, where we treat ourselves to a night at Beachcrest Inn. The proprietors there, Auburn and Trey, tell us all kinds of hidden places to visit, and we thoroughly enjoy ourselves in the town, at the Inn, and on this secret beach they hip us to, hidden away from prying eyes.

We also made a deal with Auburn and Trey to swap promo—Wilder Adventures will keep an eye out for people on the move who are headed toward the coast, and they'll keep an eye out for visitors looking for other great destinations.

On the last night, parked in the RV at Tierney Bay State Park, which has got to be the most beautiful campground on the whole Oregon coast, I say to Rachel, "So. When I suggested this cross country trip, I had ulterior motives."

She turns in my arms and runs a finger down my chest. Even though I just finished making love to her, my body stirs, ready to go another round. It's like that with Rachel. We've both been insatiable. "Getting me naked in an RV every night?"

"Well, that, yes, but beyond that. I figured if the two of us could live for two weeks together in an RV, I could make a convincing case that we'd be happy together in an 900-square-foot apartment." I shrug. "Oh. And some of the time we'd have an infant who still doesn't always sleep through the night? I promise not to make you change diapers."

"Brody. Are you asking me to move in with you?"

Her eyes glitter in the low light.

"Are you crying?" I ask, with wonder.

"Can I tell you something?" she says, sniffling. "When I was a little kid, and I played all those games? Library, wedding, house? Do you know who the groom was? The daddy? The man in the plan?"

I shake my head.

"You, Brody. It was you. It was always you."

Brody's big boat is bursting at the seams.

We're celebrating his official adoption of Justin, and the boat is full of Perezes and Wilders, a few friends from Rush Creek, Zoë and Zoë's mom, Rena, because family is family even when it's complicated.

I'm pretty sure it was the happiest moment of Brody's life when he put that pen to paper and signed his name, making it official, although when I suggested that, he frowned. He said it was tied with when I stepped back from the door of my apartment in Boston and showed him the suitcases sitting there. "That was when I knew you were mine. And now I know Justin's mine, too," he said.

On the day Brody signed the papers, we got to take Justin home with us, where we fed him cake and ice cream and danced him around the apartment and let him fall asleep in the bed between us before we lowered him gently into the real, actual crib that we'd set up in the brand new nursery.

Now Justin's running around the boat, talking up a storm to whomever will listen (everyone) about the boat and the birds and the elk and the pika and the cake—he's all about the cake—and his cousins, who are already his biggest heroes.

After a while he runs out of steam and wants Zoë, and she takes him and sits with him while we bring him gifts.

Justin's grandmothers—Barb and Zoë's mom—and his honorary abuela and bisabuelita—my mom and grandmother—are clustered around him with their gifts like the magi. Ever since Brody and I came home, the four of them have been competing for most-favored grandma status, and it's a fight to the finish, with each of them desperately trying to one-up the others—gifts, activities, food, sweets. Brody and Zoë and I do everything we can to hold back the flood of excess so Justin won't become totally spoiled.

But it's a lost cause.

Like now, for example, Caridad has a giant pink stuffed pig for him and Barb has given him a bright-colored plastic garbage truck, and Rena found shoes that squeak *and* light up when he walks, and my mom gave him one of those hand-held kiddie computers.

Brody is watching the cluster of hovering women with amusement, and when I drift to his side, he puts his arm around me and squeezes me close.

"Happy?" I ask him.

"Yeah."

As if it's not totally obvious from the fact that I haven't seen him scowl in weeks. I know some women would miss the bad-boy scowl... but I don't. Seeing Brody happy melts me inside. And there's just enough bad boy left to Brody—motorcycle included—to meet my needs.

(Plus I know exactly how to get him to scowl. It involves

putting on teeny tiny black lace panties and bra while he watches, then layering on a thick sweater and jeans. "Wait!" he says. "You're wrapping all that up?" "Yup." "Can't I lick it first?" "Busy, later!" Lots of scowls. And then, when I get my fill of grumpy Brody, I give in. Because, the licking.)

He ducks his head and nuzzles my neck, as if he can read my thoughts. "Are you exhausted?" he asks.

I was up late last night, studying for an exam. I'm getting my MSW—master of social work—degree online, as well as a certificate to be a licensed sex educator. It's basically taking the work I did helping my mom to the next level, so I can offer women even more support. And as part of that, I'm also starting my own business, selling sex toys—but not through another reseller. No, I'll be my own business, curating and choosing only the best.

When Brody heard that we'd need to do a whole bunch of testing and experimenting to find *only the best*, he was not at all bummed out.

It's been tons of fun, and the perfect counterpoint to way too much time spent hitting the books.

Amanda scoots close to me on my other side and drapes an arm. "Need a third wheel?"

"Doesn't everyone?" I ask fondly. She and Lucy and I— and Hanna, when we follow the rules—have become thick as thieves and spend loads of time together. Lucy's not here today, though, because she hates boats, and she hates them extra much now that she's pregnant and has morning (read: all-day) sickness. We found out about the pregnancy a couple of days ago—at the same time we learned that she and Gabe are engaged. Needless to say, we're all over-the-moon excited.

"Did you hear the big news?" Amanda asks.

"Wait, there's more besides Lucy being pregnant and engaged?"

She nods, eyes gleeful, and lowers her voice. "Clark has a girlfriend."

Brody's shaking his head. "No way."

"He does. I saw it with my own eyes on that glamping trip I went on with him."

Brody's eyebrows are drawn together so tight they form a monobrow. I'm with him—even though Clark no longer seems quite as stricken as he did when I first came back to Rush Creek, he's said on more than one occasion that there's no way he's ready to get back in the saddle. His brothers are super respectful of that, and I've never seen any of them try to fix him up. Amanda and his mom, not so much.

As Amanda moves along, possibly to share her gossip even further, Brody's puzzled expression smooths out a bit. "Do you think...?" he begins, then stops. "No. He wouldn't."

"What?" I demand.

"He wouldn't."

"Brody, you know that's not fair! You have to tell me."

"Well, I just—I'm just remembering this one time we talked about it and he said something..." But then he shakes his head again, and returns his attention to watching his son scoot the garbage truck along the bottom of the boat. Needless to say, Barb is preening like a peacock about the fact that her gift has "won." Until Justin grabs the shoes and shakes them and demands to have them put on his feet.

"I just have a *feel* for what little kids love," Rena tells her competitors proudly.

It's going to be a long sixteen-and-a-half years with this crew, and I'm going to love every minute of it.

Once I finish extracting intel from Brody.

I punch him in the arm. "Tell me what Clark said. Right this second." He's still a man of few words, and sometimes I have to pry every one out of him.

"He said..." Brody lowers his voice. *"If I thought it would shut Mom up? I'd get a fake girlfriend. Let me know if you find anyone who's in the market for a pretend relationship."*

"He was just kidding," I say. "Right?"

Brody and I look at each other. "He had to be. It was a long time ago, anyway. It doesn't mean anything."

But he still doesn't look sure.

It's going to be an interesting next few weeks in the Wilder family.

Not that there's ever a dull moment.

ACKNOWLEDGMENTS

I love my readers. You give me a reason to get up in the morning and a reason to put words on the page. You believe with me in the reality of the voices in my head, and you get excited with me over the little things—a new character, a new cover, a new chapter. Thank you for being my partners on this trip.

The day the Wilder brothers waltzed into my life was like a perfect meet cute—and this series is our happily ever after. I love writing about them, their heroines, and their family and friends. And of course they happened along at a moment in time—a global pandemic—when I needed, more than anything, to lose myself in story. But I couldn't possibly give birth to the Wilder Adventures by myself.

On this particular leg of the journey, I was helped immeasurably by the personal and family stories of Aimee Triana Alvarez. I met Aimee when our daughters' fourth grade teacher decided they needed to be friends. It was a great match—but the even greater match was Aimee and me. Aimee, I love you! In addition to being one of the people who saved my sanity via porch-sits during the pandemic, Aimee also generously shared with me about Cuban families, food, culture, names, and anything else I could think to ask.

I've been lucky enough to have some truly awesome helpers along the way, including my early readers this time around, Dylann Crush, Christina Hovland, Christine D'Abo, Brenda St. John Brown, Kate Davies, and Rachel Grant (AKA the one who *knows things* about boats and motorcycles). Thank you for taking time away from your own (amazing) creations to help make this book the best it could be.

Huge thanks also to the author friends who support me on a regular basis—Dylann, Megan Ryder, Christy, Brenda, Christine, Gwen Hernandez, Rachel, Kate, Kris Kennedy, Karen Booth, Susannah Nix, and many, many more, including but not limited to the authors of the Corner of Smart and Sexy, Small Town World Domination, Wide for the Win, Tinsel and Tatas, and my two ongoing newsletter swaps.

Thank you to my agent, Emily Sylvan Kim, and my sub rights agent, Tina Shen, who work to make things happen for me even when I don't know it!

Thank you, Sarah Sarai, for your copyedits, your honesty, your patience, your blessed humor... and, of course, the ellipses. Don't laugh, but I did the ellipsis in this sentence wrong the first time and had to consult the style guide.

Thank you to Sofía Ivy Pupo, who did an thorough, thoughtful, and kind sensitivity edit on this book, with guidance from Tessera Editing's Manu Shadow Velasco. I can't say enough good things about Tessera, Manu, and Sofi. But at bottom, this book is my human endeavor, for better or for worse, and any errors I have made or words that might wound or trigger, are mine and mine alone. If that happens, please let me know so I can apologize and learn to be better.

Thank you, XPresso Book Tours, especially Giselle, for the cover reveal and release support.

I cannot imagine doing any of my jobs without the love and support of my amazing friends, Aimee, Chelsea, Cheryl, Darya, Ellen, Gail, Jess, Julia, Kathy, Lauren, Molly, Soomie, and Tracey.

As Bell Girl gets ready to go off to college and Bell Boy learns to drive, I am painfully aware that my days with my kids in the house are coming to an end. But you two will always be here in my thoughts, patiently giving me time in my office except in cases of absolute emergency (reciting, "only blood, vomit, or broken glass, right, Mommy?"). I will always be surprised to come downstairs and discover you not there, waiting to ask the question you swallowed, graciously, for hours. You are my best work and also so much better than I could ever have dreamed you up. I love you.

And last, but really first, there is Mr. Bell. My best meet cute, my perfect partner, and my favorite HEA. I love you.

ALSO BY SERENA BELL

Wilder Adventures

Make Me Wilder

Walk on the Wilder Side

Wilder With You

Returning Home

Hold On Tight

Can't Hold Back

To Have and to Hold

Holding Out

Tierney Bay

So Close

So True

So Good (2022)

So Right (2023)

Sexy Single Dads

Do Over

Head Over Heels

Sleepover

New York Glitz

Still So Hot!

Hot & Bothered

Standalone

Turn Up the Heat

ABOUT THE AUTHOR

USA Today bestselling author Serena Bell writes contemporary romance with heat, heart, and humor. A former journalist, Serena has always believed that everyone has an amazing story to tell if you listen carefully, and you can often find her scribbling in her tiny garret office, mainlining chocolate and bringing to life the tales in her head.

Serena's books have earned many honors, including a RITA finalist spot, an RT Reviewers' Choice Award, Apple Books Best Book of the Month, and Amazon Best Book of the Year for Romance.

When not writing, Serena loves to spend time with her college-sweetheart husband and two hilarious kiddos—all of whom are incredibly tolerant not just of Serena's imaginary friends but also of how often she changes her hobbies and how passionately she embraces the new ones. These days, it's stand-up paddle boarding, board-gaming, meditation, and long walks with good friends.

Made in the USA
Las Vegas, NV
29 October 2021